Helter

Skelter

Rhiannon Superstar!
Thank you so much
for all your help o

By

Jo R. Brown

Work on 'Tusday'
Love Jo xx

"When I get to the bottom
I go back to the top of the slide
Where I stop and I turn and I go for a ride
Till I get to the bottom and I see you again…"

Lennon/McCartney

For Tony, who believed in me

Chapter one

My name is Jaz, it is actually Jason, but somehow, for reasons I hardly remember, it became Jaz. Something to do with a spotty boy at school who was incapable of calling anyone by their natural name, feeling compelled to alter an ordinary name into something more interesting, or just plain ridiculous. Having the name Jason, I suppose, made me a prime target for one of his 'improvements'. Anyhow, the name stuck, and for the majority of my adult life, I have been known as Jaz.

I am in my late twenties, six foot one tall, short dark hair, reasonably good looking. I have led a moderately successful life. I have my own business running the second largest comic shop in the city, a moderate income, and moderate success with the opposite sex. I have no commitments financial or otherwise, although I do have a three-year-old van, mainly for business, and a 900cc red Ducati bike.

My story begins on a glorious autumn day, with clear blue sky, white cottonwool clouds and a biting fresh breeze. I had felt rough since I had to drag my poor hungover body out of bed that morning in time to open up the shop. I had been out the previous night to a small gathering at a friends place. As usual I was in pursuit of the buxom Rachel; the lovely Rachel with her perfect face, curvaceous body, perfect hair and designer clothes. The closest I had ever come to persuading her to share my bed for a night of unbridled passion was a lingering kiss goodnight after walking her home about a month beforehand, which came to an abrupt end when she realised it was raining and her hair might get ruined. This episode left me confused and frustrated to say the least, I mean, who cares if it is raining when two consenting adults are on the brink of making sexual history. She obviously didn't see it the same way, and I am starting to think that maybe she isn't worth the effort. Especially at this very moment; having spent an evening showering Rachel with all my charm, wit and attention, to what end? A lonely bed and my head feeling like it had just been trampled over by a herd of charging rhinoceros.

I needed to get out of the shop and try to clear my head with some fresh autumn air. It was just after lunch time, the shop was relatively quiet. Mark, my twentysomething right hand man, was in, I could leave him in charge, I deserved a break anyhow.

Walking out of the shop I pondered, *do I go left into town?* No, I might bump into someone I know, and the way I feel at the moment, that is not a cheering thought. I will go up the lane and walk through the park, not the coolest hangout, but who feels cool, I asked myself. I have to admit it was a beautiful day. The leaves on the trees were a rich golden brown colour, and the sun shone through them so brightly, they almost looked as though they were on fire. The whole park seemed to glow. The grass was crisp with frost which seemed to reflect and intensify the sunlight. The sun was very low, and walking towards it I found myself almost blinded. *Why had I not worn my shades?* my poor mashed brain was moaning.

There were very few people in the park that day, much to my relief. I needed to sit down and have a cigarette. Through the trees I could see the children's play area, and a bench, now I had a sense of direction. I dropped my heavy body down on to the bench and proceeded to fumble in my pockets for my cigarettes. The bench had a layer of white frost on it and the wood had become almost black from the penetration of rainwater which made it cold and damp. In my general state of discomfort, however, this minor detail hardly seemed to matter.

I had finally located my cigarettes and pulled out of my coat pocket a packet of Marlboro. As I took a cigarette out of the packet, a young woman came up to me.
"Have you got a light?" she asked, holding a cigarette in her fingers. Her fingers were red from the cold. I looked up at her face, she had beautiful, large, pale blue eyes with heavy lashes. Her cheeks were also blushed from the cold, which gave her an astonishingly healthy glow. She had long, unkempt blonde hair. I guess she was in her late teens, maybe early twenties. She smiled at me, the most beautiful friendly smile. Her whole presence was very natural and warm, I felt instantly at ease.
"Sure, why don't you have one of these," I said, offering her a Marlboro. She took the cigarette and

leaned over for a light. She seemed petite and vulnerable leaning over my clasped hand. I felt I should put my arm around her and warm her up. There seemed to be a strange air of tragedy about her.

"Thanks," she said, smiling, almost winking her heavy eyes. She turned and walked away, drawing heavily on the cigarette.

It wasn't until then that I noticed a small child climbing over a wooden climbing frame about twenty feet from my bench. The girl was making her way over to where the child was playing. I leaned back on my bench drawing in the warm smoke from my cigarette, and started to sense some feeling in my body again. I watched the young woman and child playing together. They were running around the climbing frame chasing each other and laughing. The child couldn't have been more than two years old, I thought, though I am no expert in judging children's ages. She was wearing yellow wellington boots, a muddy red coat, hat and scarf, and oversized blue gloves. *Was she the woman's daughter?* I thought. Surely not, she seemed too young to be a mother. If she was the mother, where was the father? These were the sort of thoughts that ran over my mind as I watched them.

I finished my cigarette and looked at the time; time to head back to the shop. Brain now refreshed and in gear, it was time to return to my baby, and find out if Mark had had much business, or simply played all the CDs at full volume in defiance to my banning all music in the shop that morning due to my delicate state. I pulled myself up off the bench and glanced over at the young woman and child. They were now heading out of the park in the opposite direction to the one I would be taking. The child skipped on ahead, the young woman slowly following, jacket collar pulled up over her neck, arms tightly folded. I stood for a few seconds, wondering if she would turn around and honour me with her intoxicating smile. She didn't turn around, she kept walking away from me, intriguing me with her mystery.

I started walking back to town and realised how bitterly cold I felt. *All I need now is a strong black coffee, that should put me in gear and set me up for the day.* For the day? It was by now mid afternoon. Sure enough as I approached the shop, I could hear the deep thudding sound of the bass. *If this keeps up we'll get complaints.* It was a momentary thought, as right now I had gone beyond caring. I walked in the door, Mark was leaning over the counter looking through a comic with a customer, pointing out this and that. As usual Louise was at Mark's side, all admiring and totally devoted. Louise was supposed to be studying an economics degree, or so rumour had it, but she spent most of her life attached to Mark, in drape-like fashion. Did she have no other function in life: friends, shopping, a lecture to go to. She did have one saving grace, she made a mean cup of coffee, and a cup of coffee was at the top of my agenda.

Louise saw me come in and nudged Mark. Mark looked up at me, and quickly reached under the counter pressing the off switch on the CD player.

"Rachel phoned," he said enthusiastically, obviously pleased with himself for being the bearer of good news. Louise was a bit more in tune and suggested making us all cups of coffee. I hung my coat up in the back room, taking my cigarettes and lighter out of my pocket, and came through to the shop. Placing my cigarettes under the counter I asked Mark how the shop had been while I'd been out.

"Pretty good, sold three graphic novels, couple of posters, two books. Oh yeah, a delivery arrived. It's all signed for and it's out the back, haven't had a chance to unpack it yet. Rachel phoned." This time he conveyed the news with less enthusiasm, more curiosity. It had not received the response he'd expected, and he was obviously puzzled.

"What did she want?" I asked, not feeling particulary interested, but I felt that I had to give some response before Mark started asking probing questions about my non-existent sex life.

"She wants you to give her a ring at work, something about Saturday night." *Saturday, that is two days away, I'll ring her tomorrow.*

Louise arrived with the coffees, then proceeded to drape herself over Mark. This gave me a feeling of despair, and I suggested Mark should go and sort out the new delivery. Louise, of course followed. I wondered what would happen if they became physically separated, would they wither up and crumble, be unable to function? I took a sip of hot, strong, black coffee. Nectar to my lips. I sighed, slipping myself into the counter chair. I was beginning to warm up. Looking around at the customers browsing through the comics, I felt that maybe the place lacked a certain ambience, and sifted through the pile of CDs, looking for something appropriate.

The phone rang. I picked it up, it was Rachel.
"I rang earlier!" she said in a demanding tone.
"Yeah, I was out. How are you?" I asked, still fumbling through CDs, *this one will do*, and I inserted the disc, turning the volume down.
"Fine, I had a great time last night." *Really?* I thought. Maybe I hadn't spent the evening with Rachel after all, maybe it had all been a bad dream.
"Good, what can I do for you?" I asked, looking longingly at my cigarettes, and trying to fathom out why it is that when a person feels like death, they have this compulsive desire to abuse their body further.
"Susie's having a dinner party on Saturday night, wants to know if you can come. Niall, Rick, Emma and Phil are all invited." I had nothing else planned for that night and who knows, maybe I might get lucky with Rachel. We arranged that I'd pick her up at eight and we'd go on from there.

Had I had this episode with Rachel a week ago, or even yesterday, I would be feeling full of hope and inflated ego, as it was I felt uninterested and uninspired. I had been pursuing Rachel for too long and had become bored and disillusioned with her provocative teasing,

7

her manufactured good looks and her gossipy conversation. Though I had to admit I did still lust after her, so maybe Saturday night could be OK.

My thoughts kept drifting back to the girl in the park. Her appeal so unique, so natural, so fresh and unaffected. She was not a classic beauty and certainly didn't have the physical voluptuousness that normally appealed to me. Yet there was something almost bewitching about her presence. I could not get out of my mind the picture of her pretty face, those huge pale winking eyes, and that gorgeous smile. She had made me feel alive when I had felt like death. I wanted to see her again. I suddenly felt panic stricken. What if I never did see her again? Maybe she didn't live in the city, maybe she was just passing through. I couldn't cope with that thought. I had to find her, but how do I go about finding a girl I know absolutely nothing about?

My thoughts were interrupted by a group of young boys wanting to know how much I would pay for their dad's collection of first edition comics, which were in a carrier bag one of the boys was clutching. First editions were always valuable, especially if in good condition, so this demanded some serious attention. The end of a long day had finally arrived. Mark, Louise and Geoff, my junior member of staff, had all left and I locked up shop. I paused outside the shop and lit up a cigarette. My head felt as I imagined eggs must feel after they have been scrambled, and the feeling of relief that the day was over was overpowering. I headed home to my sanctuary.

Chapter two

My flat is rented; I do not feel the need for long-term commitments, and find comfort in the thought that if I wanted a change of scene, I could just get up and go without too much hassle. It is a good sized one-bedroom flat, with a spacious living room and two large sash windows which overlook the green and the city beyond. It is on the first floor of a large Georgian building on a slight hill, so the view is pretty impressive. It is a typical 'bachelor pad', scattered with over-full ashtrays, old coffee cups and comics! The comics are everywhere, piles on the floor, on the shelves, by the loo, in the kitchen. Boxes of comics line the hallway, in fact my flat has become an extended stockroom.

I am happy in my disorganised chaos, it feels comfortable, it makes it home. I couldn't bear to live in a sterile environment. Trudie, one of my more recent lovers, hated my flat, said it was too 'male', and proceeded to feminise it by moving in and tidying. Organisation she called it. Needless to say Trudie moved out after a few months; I lost a lover, but regained my nest. My friends like it many a happy evening has been spent with a few cans of beer, browsing through the endless supply of reading matter.

It was Saturday morning, I went through to the living room and drew open the curtains, glanced briefly out of the window, just to check that no major alterations had taken place in my view over night. Everything seemed normal. I went through to the kitchen, plugged in the kettle, and lit a cigarette. Kettle boiled, I made a strong black coffee and sat down with coffee and cigarette.

I felt great, I had a really good feeling about today, Saturdays were always busy days at work, which of course meant more money. I am going out to dinner tonight, so no need to worry about feeding myself, and the icing on the cake, I was going to get laid. Yes, I felt sure that tonight was the night that I would finally seduce Rachel.

The phone rang, I could hear it but I couldn't see it. I looked under the comics on the sofa next to me, no luck, under the cushions, no, try the bedroom. I walked through to the bedroom, there was a pile of clothes on the floor by the bed, I looked underneath, there was the phone.

"Hello."

"Jaz, hi, it's Niall, how's it going mate?"

"Pretty cool."

"Could you take a break today, meet up in the pub at lunch time?" Niall asked.

"No, sorry mate, Saturdays are really busy, if I left Mark in charge on a Saturday he would lose half the stock to shoplifters. Stop by the shop though, and I'll make you a coffee."

"Cheers Jaz, I'll do that. I admire your dedication to your business. Are you going to Susie's bash tonight?"

"Yes, I have a good feeling about tonight."

"Oh yeah, and how's it going with Rachel?"

"Don't ask, look I've got to go and open up the shop, I'll fill you in later. I need your advice on something."

"Sounds interesting, I'll see you later."

I arrived at the shop where Geoff, Mark and, of course, Louise were all waiting outside. I felt like asking Louise if she worked here, then thought of the coffee she was inevitably about to make for me, and thought better of it. Everyone entered the shop, coats off, lights on, music on, pick up the post off the floor.

"Everyone for coffee?" Louise cheerfully asked. The question was merely a formality, the answer being a foregone conclusion. Just then the door crashed open; it was Sarah, my enthusiastic Saturday girl, who spent most of her life taking Ecstasy and going to raves.

"Sorry I'm late, Jaz. Hi everybody. You'd do well to stay open late tonight, Father Christmas is coming to town." I looked at her strangely. *She's still going from last night,* I thought.

"Jaz, don't give me one of those disapproving looks. The Christmas lights, Father Christmas is coming to town to turn the Christmas lights on, there'll be loads of people about, they might want to do some shopping." No doubt about it, the girl was on drugs. Now how do I break it to her gently that Father Christmas doesn't exist.

"Christmas lights, it's the middle of November for Christ's sake!" I exclaimed.

"It was just a thought!" Sarah replied in an indignant manner, continuing through to the back of the shop to hang up her coat. Louise arrived with the coffees, and the customers came in. The morning whizzed by, trade was good. The bright sunlight flooded through the large shop windows. The inside of the shop felt warm and comfortable, which was no bad thing because it meant that once the customers were in, they were reluctant to go back out into the cold.

The shop was busy, Mark and myself were serving at the counter, Geoff and Sarah were restacking shelves, keeping an eye out for shoplifters and dealing with general enquiries. It was a good day. I looked up to serve the next customer and saw Niall waiting at the side. I acknowledged him and called Geoff over to serve.

"Niall, how are you? Come out the back I'll make us a coffee." Niall and I slipped out the back, I grabbed my packet of Marlboro on the way. I put on the kettle and surveyed the mess of coffee granules and sugar on the work surface. "Jesus, Louise!" I exclaimed under my breath.

"So, interesting conversation we had on the phone this morning," said Niall in a leading, quizzical manner. "Niall, I met this girl, well I sort of met her. I can't shake her out of my head. It's driving me nuts, I've got to see her again."

"Woah, slow down mate. I presume we are not talking about the lovely Rachel?" Niall replied in a calming manner. I proceeded to fill Niall in on the meeting I had in the park with the young woman and child.

"What do I do, Niall? I mean, how do I go about meeting someone I know nothing about?"

"Well, let's survey the facts first of all. She's a young attractive woman. She has a daughter."

"I don't know if the child was hers," I interrupted.

"OK," Niall replied, "but let's presume at the moment that she is. People with children take their children to places they can play and have fun."

"OK, so you suggest I hang out in parks and puppet theatres?" I replied sarcastically.

"I don't know, let's have a cigarette and a think."

We sat in thoughtful silence for a moment, smoking and drinking our coffees.

"You do realise of course, that if the child is hers, there has to be a father somewhere," Niall added.

"Maybe the child isn't hers, she could have been babysitting it. Maybe she childminds as a job," I suggested hopefully. Niall wasn't listening, he had gone into detective mode, I could almost see the cogs in his brain whizzing around at ferocious speed.

"Christmas lights!" he exclaimed, enthusiastically. Not Niall too, had everyone gone completely crazy today, was I the only sane being left?

"No, listen!" he said with excitement. I looked at him expecting him to leap up and down and produce a carefully written present list addressed to Father Christmas. "If the child is hers, she'll more than likely take her to see the lights tonight. It'll be packed out so you could mingle with the crowd, find her, suss out whether she's on her own, or with a fella. If she's on her own, then all systems go, if she's with a ten foot muscle man you make a discreet exit, and lose nothing."

Nothing but a dream, I thought. Niall's plan seemed plausible enough, but how was I to find her in a massive crowd of people and excited children?
"No Niall, really, Christmas lights, Father Christmas. It's just so uncool."
"Well, it was only a suggestion, Jaz. If you ask me you'd be better off focusing on Rachel. Mate, you have got her exactly where you want her now, she is putty in your hands. Tonight she'll be all over you, you wouldn't be able to keep her out of your bed with an army. Take my word for it." Niall obviously had some inside information, probably from Susie, Niall's sometime girlfriend, and Rachel's best friend and confidant. Why is it when I try so hard to get a woman into bed, she doesn't want to know, then, when I lose interest, she is ready to pounce?

It was time to get back to the front of the shop, and for Niall to continue on his Saturday meanderings. I mulled over Niall's advice for a few hours. Rachel was a definite possibility, and after all I had waited so long, it seemed a waste to give up now. I really had lost the desire I had previously had for her, but I really could do with a night full of sexual passion. The young woman in the park held a different sort of desire, a much deeper desire, physical yes, but there was more to it than that. Intrigue. I felt confused, I had been thinking about it all too much. I would go to Rachel's as previously arranged, and go on to the dinner party as planned.

The day was over, I locked up the shop, lit my cigarette, and proceeded to head home. I didn't work far from home, I could take the short, usual walk, which skirted the city centre, or I could cut through town, which was slightly longer but enabled me to do any last minute shopping I had to do. I was going to head straight home, then paused surveying the hoards of people heading to town, presumably to see the lights being turned on. I could go to the off licence and get a couple of bottles of wine for tonight, I convinced myself. That was a grand plan, I congratulated myself, going to the off licence meant going to town and walking straight past the place 'Father Christmas' would be. I had an ulterior motive and if I just happened to 'bump' into the gorgeous young woman then all the better.

The crowds were heaving, it was freezing and dark. Father Christmas had not yet arrived and the children were all very excited about his imminent appearance. There were carol singers singing, hot chestnut stands, fun fair rides and a noisy procession making its way slowly down the main street. "It is only November!" I muttered to myself in disbelief. I kept an eye out for the young woman as I squeezed my way through the crowds, but really had little hope of seeing her, if she was even here in the first place.

Suddenly there was pandemonium, whistles and trumpets blew, and the whole crowd seemed to be shifted ever tighter and closer together. Father Christmas, or should I say a man dressed in ridiculous red clothes with bits of white fluff attached to them, a big false white beard and a silly red hat with a huge white pom-pom on the end, had arrived. I had to get out of the crowd. I checked my pocket to see if my cigarettes were still intact and not crumpled in the wrestling. They were, I realised, with a great sense of relief. I managed to squeeze my way out of the crowd into a shop doorway, where I hastily pulled out a cigarette and lit it up. I would stay here until it was all over.

Slowly dragging on the cigarette, I noticed a small child on top of someone's shoulders quite a way in front in the crowd. She was wearing a hat and scarf, muddy red coat, and I thought I could just make out a pair of yellow wellington boots. It was the child I had seen with the young woman, she was here, I had to get closer. There was little chance of that, the crowd was packed solid. I fixed my eyes on the child, as soon as she moved I would follow. Time seemed to be passing in slow motion. I felt as though I had been standing here for hours. I had smoked at least three cigarettes. Then it happened, the crowd seemed to be dispersing. I kept my eyes on the child, as the crowd became thinner, the child suddenly got down from the adult's shoulders. How was I to find them now? I walked quickly in the direction I last saw them heading in. I had lost them. I felt deflated and shuffled along the pavement looking at the ground.

"Freya, come here babe." I was sure I recognised that voice. I know I had only heard her speak once, but I was sure it was the young woman's voice. I looked in the direction of the voice, and sure enough, there she was. She was wearing a hip-length jacket, the collar of which she had pulled up over her neck, and a short, pretty, flowery, flirty skirt, or was it a dress? She had dark tights, and flat-heeled boots. Hardly the expensive fashionable attire Rachel would wear, but she looked absolutely stunning. She seemed to be on her own. I pushed my way through the crowd and ran over to her. She was tickling the child and they were both laughing, she swung the child around, and as she stopped she looked up. She stared straight at me and smiled. That smile was so warm and wonderful I actually stopped in my tracks. Had she recognised me? She turned and walked away. I walked up to her.

"Hello." I said to her.
"Hi." she replied, smiling, but without recognition.
"I saw you in the park the other day, I gave you a cigarette. Maybe you don't remember. I probably looked pretty awful, I had a dreadful hangover." She didn't reply, simply looked at me with her huge pale eyes and smiled.
I had to do something, I was in danger of making a complete fool of myself. She looked cold. I could really do with a coffee and she looked as though she could too.
"Could I buy you a coffee? It's pretty cold out here, we could go to a cafe and warm up?" I suggested.

"OK," she replied, favouring me with yet more knockout smiles.

There was a cafe quite close by, that I knew made a reasonable cup of coffee. I held open the door for her and she and the child walked in. She found an empty table with two fixed benches, one either side. She took off the child's coat and hat, and the little girl slid along the bench to the end next to the wall. She then took off her jacket, and shook her long hair free, and sat down.
"What would you like to drink?" I asked, trying desperately to keep my cool. She asked for a black coffee and offered me some money to get the child a sandwich and glass of milk. I walked up to the counter in a state of shock. I had actually done it, I had found her, I was going to sit down in her company and talk to her. My heart was racing.

"Yes, please!"
A loud and aggressive voice pierced into my thoughts. I looked up and faced a large scowling middle-aged woman who had been waiting for me to order for some time.

Chapter three

I carried the tray over to the table and put it down. I then proceeded to hand the coffee to the young woman, and sandwich to the child. She helped me offload the things which were left on the tray, looking up with her winking, smiling eyes, and thanked me. The child started rearranging the contents of her egg and salad sandwich over the table top. The young woman coolly put the food back on the plate and asked the child to eat up.

I sat down opposite her and looked at her lovely face. Her healthy complexion had not changed. Her long, ash blonde hair had a tousled appearance. It seemed to have been haphazardly layered, her fringe stood up away from her face in no particular direction, the whole appearance of which gave her a natural 'just got out of bed look'. There was something extraordinarily sexy about her, but it was very subtle, there was nothing obvious.

"What's your name?" I asked, too impatient for small talk.
"What's yours?" she replied, in a teasing manner.
"Jaz."
"Katie."
I gestured over to the child. "Her name is Freya. The name comes from the old Norse name of the Goddess of love."

"Is she yours?" I enquired, trying to sound casual.

"She's my babe," Katie replied, giving the child a cuddle, Freya giggled. I wondered if the mother had been the inspiration for the name.

We chatted and laughed together for some time, though it seemed as though no time had passed at all. I told her about my shop; she said she had heard of it but never visited. I, of course, gave her an open invitation. Apart from that we just talked about nothing in particular; she gave me no details about herself or her life, and I didn't ask. The conversation flowed so naturally, enquiring questions didn't seem appropriate, or even, at the time, important. I found her company very relaxed and easy. I didn't feel the need to impress, or flatter her, as I would most women. She felt like an instant friend. I was totally at ease with her. I also desired her, as I had never desired anyone before. She was small and looked vulnerable, I wanted to hold her, kiss her, make love to her. What was most extraordinary of all, was that I felt I could. She had put up no barriers, she seemed very open. She was not playing games or teasing; she just was. Our conversation was interrupted by the arrival of a young man.

"Hi, Katie." He sat down next to Katie, sliding his body up against hers gently pushing her along the bench towards Freya. He put his arm in a confident manner around the back of the bench behind Katie and kissed her on the check. She looked up at me with her heavy eyes and smiled a reassuring smile.

"Hi, Miles," Katie said, with a hint of laughter in her voice. The man was of medium height and build, probably about my age. He sat with a slouch, his pelvis thrust forward, and his legs spread wide apart. His presence was very confident, almost cocky. He was wearing an oversized dark coat, buttons undone, a green baggy jumper and dark jeans. His brown hair was collar length and looked as though it may have had a style some years previously, but had now forgotten what it was supposed to be.

"How's it going, Katie, how are you doing, Freya?" he said leaning over in front of Katie to address the child. "We see Father Chrissmas," Freya replied without looking up from the sandwich she was concentrating very hard on holding, and coordinating into her mouth.

"Oh yeah, I hope you had a good time. Did he switch the lights on?" said Miles. He then focused his attention on Katie. "Are you going to The Dome tonight, babe?"

"Yes, I am, are you?" she replied in a nonchalant manner.

"Oh Katie, I've just seen H. He's looking for you, he was down by the fountain with Carl," Miles added.

I knew an H once, from my school days. His real name was Hugh, and yes, you guessed it, he too became a victim of the same spotty school boy, who changed his name from Hugh to H. He was the eldest son of wealthy parents. I had heard through the grapevine that he had lived up to his name-sake, and become a heroin user, possibly even addict, and had consequently been disowned by his wealthy family. Could this man possibly be referring to the same H?

"I've got to go," said Katie, with a look of slight annoyance on her face. She took Freya's hand, and what was left of the disembowelled sandwich, got up and squeezed past Miles. She reached for Freya's coat, scarf, hat and gloves, dressed her, reached for her own coat and left the cafe without a word. Miles, arms and legs still spread out as though he were trying to see just how much of the bench he could cover with his body, followed her with his eyes admiringly.

"She is the coolest cat in town," he said, eyes still focused on the door she had just exited through. Then he looked at me, smiling in a knowing way. "She never says goodbye, and she's not for keeps, you'll see. You'll spend the night with her, and the next day she'll be gone. She's a law unto herself and she answers to no-one," he paused thoughtfully, "H wouldn't know a good thing if it supersonically jet-propelled itself into his main vein. Hey mate, d'you want to buy some whiz?"

"No," I replied.

I found Miles' company intrusive and exhausting, and I really ought to be going. I felt I could probably find out a lot from Miles about Katie, but I wasn't sure whether I was ready for his interpretation. I stood up, curtly said goodbye, and left the cafe. I headed off towards the off licence somewhat confused. I had had a great time with Katie. Fantastically I had managed to find her, find out her name, spend some time in her company, all had gone brilliantly. That was until Miles had turned up. Then she had suddenly left. Why did she had to leave so quickly and what role did H have in her life? I presume that it is the same H I knew of, judging by Miles' comments. Besides, just how many H's could there be in one city? Miles seemed to be quite intimate with her. What was their relationship I wondered, slightly enviously?

I reached the off licence. I bought two bottles of wine, several packets of Marlboro, left and lit a cigarette. I looked at my watch, it was eight thirty. Where had the time gone? I was late. I found a telephone box and dialled Rachel's number.

"Rachel, it's Jaz."

"Jaz, you're late, where have you been? I've been phoning your flat for ages."

"Sorry, look I'm in town, I got held up. I'll explain later. I'll be at your place in about five minutes."

"OK, you do realise we're half an hour late already. This is so unlike you, Jaz, you're normally so punctual!"

"Like I said, I got held up, I'll be there soon." I put the phone down. I felt slightly irritated by this conversation, probably because I felt guilty for being late, also because Rachel was right, I am always punctual. I have never been late for anything in my life. Mr Dependable, that was me. How was it then that Katie, a girl I hardly knew, had managed to distract me enough to be late for a date? I was finding the power this girl was having over me extraordinary.

We arrived at Susie's at around eight forty-five. Rachel had been quizzing me all the way about my lateness, I had so far been successfully evasive. Rachel looked lovely in a black velvet evening dress, complete with low neckline and exposed cleavage. She really had gone to a lot of effort, her appearance would normally have excited me, yet tonight the effect was minimal.

"Come on in," Susie greeted us as she opened the front door. I gave my apologies about the lateness of our arrival and went inside. Everyone was already there, drinking and chatting. I suddenly felt strangely out of place. Everyone was happy and friendly, but I didn't feel relaxed. I didn't want to be here, I wanted to be with Katie, laughing and talking. I wanted to find out more about her. She was new, she was exciting, a challenge. There was no challenge here in this room. I knew virtually everything there was to know about these people. Even Rachel's appeal had been purely physical if I was to be brutally honest, and somehow even that seemed to have passed.

I opened up one of the bottles of wine and poured Rachel and I a drink. Niall came up to me.

"Jaz, what happened to you two? Anything exciting?" he asked quietly.

"Niall, I found her, I went to town and I saw her. We had coffee together," I paused, "and then she left."

"Left!" Niall replied.

"She just got up and left. I think she had to meet someone." Niall laughed with excitement at the news of my meeting.

"So, how did it go, what's she like, does she have a name?"

"Her name is Katie, she is as wonderful as I imagined her to be. I feel so relaxed with her. We just laughed and talked about nothing in particular."

"Are you going to see her again?" Niall asked.

"I hope so," I replied thoughtfully, though I didn't know how I was ever going to see her again. I still didn't know that much about her. I didn't know where she lived or worked, or if she worked, or even if she was, in fact, single.

"I know that she is going to The Dome tonight. I overheard her arranging to meet someone there," I said remembering her conversation with Miles.

"What about Rachel?" Niall asked, "Is she out of the picture now?"

"Guess so." Just then Rachel came over to us.

"Are you two going to sit down, I think the food's ready?" she asked in a flirty voice, and took my arm.

The food was wonderful. Susie had cooked a feast of Mexican cuisine. The presentation was beautiful, very colourful, even down to the napkins and candles which were colour coordinated. For about an hour I managed to almost forget about Katie, enjoying the food and wine, laughing with my friends. Niall was uncorking probably the thirteenth bottle of wine when Emma said, "I saw Abigail yesterday, and she was saying how good The Dome was these days, can you believe it, a dive like that? Apparently it's changed hands. Gus, who used to run Sparks is running it now. It's supposed to be really happening." Niall looked at me knowingly.

There was no question about it, I had to go there. I told everyone I had a terrible headache, made my heartfelt apologies, thanked Susie for the wonderful spread and left. Niall followed me out to the door.

"Take care mate, and keep me posted."

"I will," I replied, "Look I'm really sorry about tonight."

"Get away with you," Niall replied, giving me a friendly push out of the door.

Chapter four

It was eleven-thirty as I headed towards town. *What an earth was I doing*, I asked myself in disbelief? I had just left a lovely meal and my friends, to walk into town, in the middle of a cold November night, to go to a seedy nightclub, to find a girl I hardly knew. I hadn't visited The Dome for about two years, and then infrequently. It was referred to as 'the flea pit' on account of its reputation as a seedy run-down establishment for losers. Had Gus really managed to transform the place into somewhere desirable? I doubted it. As I approached The Dome I could hear loud music pounding onto the streets. There was a huge queue of people outside waiting to go in, I joined, it seemed to be moving fairly fast. There were some people I recognised, mainly people who came to the shop, but I couldn't see Katie.

I eventually got inside. It was certainly better than I remembered it. It had had a coat of paint and seemed bright and fresh. The Dome was a large Edwardian building, probably built as a picture house originally, and then, as with so many similar buildings, became redundant with the invention of the television. When I had been there before it had been very open plan, with seating around the walls and a huge dance floor in the centre. That had all changed. It now seemed to have been carved up into lots of smaller rooms, giving it a more intimate feel. Each room had its own bar, and each were painted a different colour. Some rooms had tables and chairs, others had sofas and coffee tables. There was a large room with a dance floor that seemed to be in middle of all the others, so that it was possible to get to the dance floor from each room. This was a definite improvement, I was impressed. Judging by the heaving masses of people, the feeling was universal.

I went to the bar to buy a drink before I looked for Katie. I was standing at the bar, about to light my cigarette, when someone yelled my name. I turned around, it was Sarah, my Saturday girl.
"Jaz, how are you? Didn't expect to see you here."
"It's not bad is it. Can I buy you a drink?"
"Got one thanks. Are you on your own?"
"Sort of, I'm looking for someone."
"Anyone I might know?"
I had to think about my answer, if she did know Katie she may be able to tell me where I could find her. Then again I wasn't sure I wanted Sarah to know that I was looking for her.

I decided to play it cool and said that she wouldn't know my 'friend'. I walked around the club, wandering from room to room, with no success. Maybe she hadn't come after all, maybe she had simply told Miles she would be here so that he would not harass her. I walked through to the dance floor, stood by the wall and lit up another cigarette.
"Have you got a light?" I heard a familiar, softly spoken, voice ask.

"Hello," I said excitedly. It was Katie. "Sure, here have a cigarette too."

I fumbled about getting her a cigarette out of my Marlboro packet. She put the cigarette coolly in her mouth and leant closer to my lighter. She then drew in a deep lung full of smoke and slowly blew it out, eyes half closed, head tilted slightly back, with a look of pure enjoyment.

"How are you?" she asked smiling.

"Great, I've not been here since it changed hands, it's not bad is it?" I was standing talking to Katie, I didn't care where I was.

"It's great, but I come here too much," she replied, casually.

"Where's Freya tonight?" I asked.

"She's with a friend. I've got to get a drink," she replied and turned to go.

Maybe I shouldn't have pried; she didn't seem open to talking about her personal life.

"I'll buy you a drink. What do you want?" I offered. I couldn't lose her again. I went to the bar and as I came back I saw Miles talking to her, he took a drag of her cigarette, and sauntered off into the crowd.

She smiled as I came back with the drinks, thanking me casually. She had a very distant, cool manner about her. It was not unfriendly, more preoccupied. I wondered what her thoughts were.

"I love this song, do you want to dance?" she said smiling and winking her eyes.

"No, but I'll hold your drink if you like," I suggested.
"Thanks," she smiled and passed me her drink. I stood by the side and watched. She was totally unselfconscious and so sexy. She appeared happy with herself, and had an air of total self confidence. It was only a couple of seconds before she had a dancing partner.

She came back for her drink after the song had finished, followed by her 'dancing partner'.
"Cheers, I just love that song," she said and took her drink. The guy who had followed her back from the dance floor put his arms around her waist from behind and was teasing her. She gave me a look as if to say 'He's only a friend'.
"Get off, Matt," she said, laughing, trying to unclasp his grip.
"Come home with me," he pleaded teasingly.
"No!" she replied and gently pushed him away. He made an impression of a wounded animal and skulked off. She offered no explanation, but carried on drinking. I felt like asking her if she often received proposals like that, then thought that at this stage it really was none of my business.

"Would you like to come outside and get some fresh air?" she asked me.
Hey, I was going anywhere she wanted to go tonight. We walked out of the club. Katie seemed to know a lot of the people in the club that night, judging by the amount of people who stopped to chat to her on the way out. Some greeted her with a casual kiss, some

were just friendly. It became clear very quickly that this girl was not short of admirers, and I felt flattered that she was devoting most of her attention to me tonight.

We got outside; it was bitterly cold. She only had her thin hip-length jacket, so I offered her my thick coat. She gratefully accepted.

"What a beautiful clear night," she said gazing up at the sky. I had to admit that I hadn't really noticed, but looking up it certainly was very clear. The moon was full and the night sky looked very light.

"There's the wishing star, we must make a wish," she said gently taking hold of my hands and bringing them close to her chest. Her eyes were closed, and she had a look of concentration on her face. I just gazed at her beauty with wonderment, and thought, 'I have all that I wish for right here in front of me.'

She opened her huge pale eyes and looked up at me smiling, still holding my hands close to her. I leant forward and kissed her on the lips. She didn't seem to mind, and I kissed her again more passionately, this time with my arms around her, holding her close to my body. She felt wonderful, perfect. I wanted to whisk her off to my bed there and then. We stopped kissing and she took hold of my hand, and started running, laughing.

"Let's go to the park!" she suggested, excitedly.

"But it's the middle of the night!" I protested.

"So!" she replied, smiling, letting go of my hand and running off in the direction of the park. I ran after her.

Shortly we arrived at the park. It was very quiet and empty, but seemed strangely magical in the bright moonlight. She jumped on a swing and started swinging. I stood by her not knowing quite what to do. As the swing reached its highest peak, she jumped off laughing. She pulled me gently towards her and kissed me.

"It's such fun!" she protested. She made me feel as though I had no idea of fun, somehow she had made me feel the fool. "Come and catch me," she called, running up a hill. I chased after her, she had climbed to the top of a climbing frame and was standing on the top. I climbed up to her, out of breath, but happy. "Come and stand next to me," she cried. I stood up next to her, and she held my hand. "Now jump," she said, smiling. We held hands and jumped, landing on the soft ground on our hands and knees, laughing. She lay down on her back, I leaned over her and kissed her passionately again. This time she pushed me, teasingly, away. "Follow me," she called, and was running over to two huge swing-like objects. "You get on that one, Jaz," she said as she climbed on the other one.

They were large flat circles of wood with a single hole in the centre through which a long thick rope was attached, the other end of the rope being attached to the massive frame which supported them. The idea was to swing in a rotating manner. We had fun pushing each others swing away with our feet, each of us would swing around in a dizzy circular motion away from the other, then as we swung back towards each other one of us would push the other away with our feet, which would then send both swings rotating outwards again. I never dreamt I would be in a park in the middle of the night playing on swings. I had to admit it was great fun though.

We eventually stopped messing around in the park and I invited Katie to come back to my flat. She accepted my invitation and we headed home. It was by now approximately three in the morning. We walked back with my arm around Katie, holding her body close to mine, smoking Marlboros. I was a very happy man.

Chapter five

I woke up to the phone ringing. *Where was it?* I was thinking vaguely to myself. I hunted under a pile of clothes next to the bed and found it.

"Hello," I said, sleepily.

"Jaz, did I wake you? I was just ringing to see how you were. I was worried about you last night. Shall I come round?" It was Rachel.

I rubbed my eyes. *What time was it?* I felt as though I hadn't been to bed yet.

"No, yes, I'm fine. What time is it?" I asked trying to get my brain into gear.

"It's half past one."

"In the morning?"

"Jaz! You sure you're OK? Look I'll come round."

I was slowly starting to wake up; I looked next to me in the bed. There she was, fast asleep, Katie. The previous night's adventures slowly began to come back to me.

"No, no don't do that Rachel. There's really no need. I'm fine. I just need some sleep and a quiet day. Thanks for your concern, I'll ring you in a couple of days." and hung up. I leant back in the bed, turned and looked at Katie sleeping peacefully. She was a picture of beauty. There was none of the smudged makeup that I had come to expect from most women first thing in the morning. Maybe she didn't wear makeup.

I decided to get up and make some coffee. I quietly crept out of the bedroom so as not to wake her, and made my way to the kitchen. I put the kettle on and lit the first cigarette of the day. I went through to the living room and drew open the curtains. It was an overcast grey day and looked as though it might rain. I collected up the old ashtrays and coffee cups that had been lying around for days, and took them to the kitchen. I had a guest. I must make a bit of an effort to make the place look respectable.

The kettle boiled and I filled the cafetiere with water on top of the mountain of ground coffee I had already put in. I found a tray and placed the coffee and two cups onto it, and returned to the bedroom. Katie roused as I entered. I placed the tray next to the bed, and drew open the curtains.

"Umm, what a lovely smell," Katie said, dreamily, eyes half open. I leaned over her and gave her a gentle kiss. She opened her eyes wide and smiled. "Good morning," she said, softly.

I poured out the coffees, handed one to her, and offered her a cigarette. There we were both sitting up in bed together smoking our cigarettes and drinking our coffee.

"I had a great time last night," I said, finally waking up.

"Me too," she replied. She then reached into her coat pocket and pulled out a small paper wrap. "Would you like a line?" she asked, reaching for a hand mirror I had lying on the floor by the bed.

"What is it?" I replied.

"Coke," she answered, smiling, and proceeded to open the wrap and cut up two large lines of white powder with a razor blade.

I had not much experience with drugs, I was what might be referred to as a party drug taker in as much as I have only ever had drugs at parties, and not much at that. But I thought, why not, it's here, it's free, it could be a laugh.

"Have you got a note?" Katie asked. I handed her a fairly crisp ten pound note, which she then carefully rolled into a tube. She put one end into one of her nostrils, while pushing the other nostril closed, and with the other end close to the mirror took a large sniff. With one sniff, a line of cocaine had gone in an instant. She leaned her head back, pinched her nose, and again holding the other nostril closed took another powerful sniff. She handed me the mirror, on which the other line sat waiting. I took the ten pound note and snorted at the line, got half way through, and had to come up for air. I then lent over and finished the rest of the powder off. Katie took the mirror out of my hand, and with a wetted finger, picked up the little dust which was left, and rubbed it onto her gums. Well, what a great way to start the day I thought. Katie got out of bed, and, completely naked, proceeded to go through to the living room.

"Can I put some music on?" she called through.
"Sure." She sifted through the chaotic heap of CDs, found one she liked and put it on, turning up the

volume almost full. She then returned holding a bottle of champagne and two glasses.

"I found this in your kitchen, could we open it?" she asked seductively. Why not, I had the bottle lying around for a while and this seemed as good an occasion as any to open it. So we spent the whole day in bed, drinking champagne, snorting cocaine, listening to loud music, smoking cigarettes and making love. Outside the rain pelted down on the window pane, and the wind was blowing through the branches of the trees. I was exceedingly happy to be where I was right now.

I still didn't know much about Katie's life and wanted to know more.

"Tell me about Freya," I asked, her head lying on my shoulder, my arm around hers, both smoking cigarettes.

"She's my daughter, and she's brilliant," she replied dreamily.

"Where is she now, do you have to pick her up?"

"No, she's with a friend," she replied, becoming slightly agitated. She started to move away from me.

"Hey, what's wrong?" I asked, pulling her gently back towards me. I could see tears welling up in her eyes. She took a large drag on a cigarette.

"It's none of your business," she replied in a defensive manner. She had managed to hold back the tears, and appeared suddenly very cold. "I've got to go," she said, sadly, without looking at me.

"Don't go, I really didn't mean to upset you. I like you a lot, I want to know more about you."

"Why, why do you want to know more about me? Can't you just accept me as me. Nothing else matters right now except us in this room! What's out there is shit. And what I am to Freya, or anyone else is nothing to do with you. What I am now, with you, is all you should be concerned about. Don't spoil things. I don't ask you questions about your life. Your life is private, and I respect that. You should respect that of me too, otherwise we can't be friends."

"But Katie if I am to have a relationship with you I need to know more about you. I want to know about you, to understand you, to know who you are. I know nothing about you, your surname, where you live, how old you are."

"Why do you need to know these things, so you can catalogue me inside your brain, put me in a convenient compartment? Sorry mate, but I don't play those games. We've had a good time together, a special time, our time. That's the way it should be, why complicate things with talk of relationships? I don't want a relationship, I don't need a relationship. Life is about living, how can you live if you're constantly in the shadow of someone else?"

She got dressed, took a cigarette and left. I was left dumb struck. We had spent all day in bed, drunk a whole bottle of champagne, gone through at least a gram of cocaine, and three packets of cigarettes. I got out of bed and ran a bath. What had gone wrong? I stood by the window looking out over the green while the bath water was running. It was very dark outside. Although the moon was probably full, the sky was filled with cloud and it was raining heavily, which made the evening appear darker than it was. I looked at all the street lights and the windows of all the houses lit up. I could see people in the streets running with their umbrellas, battling against the strong wind. Town beyond, looked alive and busy. She was out there somewhere; had she gone to a friend, home, or was she just walking in the streets getting wet and cold?

The bath was ready. I got in and submerged myself in the hot steaming water. Resting my head on the bath, I lit up a cigarette. I was going to have to go and get some more, I only had a couple left.

My body was consumed with such a cocktail of toxins, I was really in no fit state to think about anything rationally, least of all the recent episode in my life. Still I tried to make sense of it all. It seemed that if I was to have any sort of relationship with Katie it would have to be on her terms. She had obviously played this game before, and I felt way out of my depth. *Why was she so secretive? Did she have some terrible secret to hide, or was she just being honest, and really meant the things she said?* I could agree with her philosophy to a certain extent, but found it difficult to see how it could work in the real and complicated world of emotions.

Enough for today, I thought. Remember the day for all the good things that happened, they far outweighed the bad. An early night I think. With that conclusion I finished in the bath, turned off the lights, and crashed out.

Chapter six

The alarm clock went off at eight o'clock on Monday morning. I felt surprisingly good, maybe due to the cocaine. I had half an hour to get up, make some coffee and get out of the flat. I opened up the curtains, the weather hadn't improved since yesterday. For all that had gone wrong, I felt very pleased with myself. I had had a wonderful time with Katie, the best ever. I didn't care what terms she lay down, I would be her devoted lover. Maybe she would come in the shop today, kiss and make up, and spend another night of wild passion with me.

I got to the shop at eight fifty-five, as Mark and Geoff were waiting outside.

"Good morning boys. No Louise today?" I said to Mark.

"She doesn't work here, Jaz. She's gone to a lecture!" Mark retorted indignantly.

"Oh, really!" I replied sarcastically, maybe I should charge her rent. Lights, music, kettle on. It was work as normal. A delivery arrived and I sent Geoff out to the back to unpack it, while I scanned the shelves to see what needed topping up. "We're low on Judge Dredd, 2000AD, Gang of Four," and so it went on as I called out the titles to Mark, who in turn made notes on pieces of paper.

I was happy to be in familiar surroundings, being distracted by my work. All the time thinking, *She's going to come into the shop at any minute, I just know it.* We have a strange mixture of people as our customers. We get the teenagers with their spotty faces, and long, greasy hair and leather jackets with 'Metallica' sprawled across the back. Some of them seem to have an endless supply of cash to spend, large allowances from their parents no doubt. While others stand awkwardly at the counter counting piles of ten and twenty pence pieces. I sometimes get overcome with pity for the latter, as they look up at me in dispair because they are five pence short of the correct amount, and let them off. What the hell, it's only five pence to me. To them, their whole happiness at that moment depends upon them leaving the shop with their prized possession. We also get the trendies, and the art students. The trendies come in wearing their latest fashions, posing around the shop. I suppose I should feel flattered that they seem to think it's such a cool hangout. The art students are not much different except in their dress, which appears to be a more 'thrown together' look consisting of garments which have just been rescued from the local charity shop. They veer towards the graphic novels, and works of 'superior artwork'.

Other interesting customers are the slightly older people, parents who browse through the shop. I never know if they are shopping for their children, or themselves. They usually come in during the lunch hour, or at the end of the day. They are probably the biggest spenders. We also get the 'hippies': There are two types of these. There are the together, mellow hippies who are always good for a chat, with some far-out new age story to tell. Then there are the other type. The ones which are drugged up to the eyeballs most of the time, who wander aimlessly around the shop, and manage to stay in the shop long enough to read a complete comic without spending a penny.

Then we get the 'ravers', who always walk in a strange way, I've noticed. They never quite stand still. I get the feeling they're probably still dancing from the night before. All those hours high on Ecstasy, dancing to remixed musical rhythms, it's probably not surprising. They must, after all, spend more time dancing than anything else.

Strangest of all though are the ones in suits, who always look terribly respectable, with their immaculate hair cuts, pressed shirts and ties, briefcases and serious faces. I wonder if these are how train spotters become when they grow up. Last, but not least, the children. I dread three-thirty every day. School's finished and they appear in hoards. Then they all crowd around one comic, making lots of noise. Dumping their bags in the gangway, leaving their gum on the floor. It feels like a plague of locusts some days. All of them pay the bills so, as far as I'm concerned, they are all wonderful. Comics are my passion, so if they are someone else's too, then good for them.

I have been running the shop now for almost five years. I started off with a loan from my family which I repay on a monthly basis at a low rate of interest. I moved to these premises three years ago. The previous shop became too small, and was not in quite the right location. The location of this shop is much more central. Also, it is on quite a major road with lots of similar type shops.

Mark has been with me since just before we changed premises, Louise has been with us since she and Mark became glued together about two years ago. Mark is a dependable, uncomplicated guy who likes nothing better than spending an evening with Louise reading a good graphic novel. He is twenty five years old, content with life, has bought a small flat, and goes to the odd gig. Geoff is probably the most recent member of staff. He has been here almost a year. I have not quite sussed Geoff out yet. He is also very dependable and obviously loves his job. He is quite a sociable character and has lots of student-type friends popping in to visit. He graduated from university last year with a 2.1, but then decided he had studied the wrong degree. I think basically Geoff doesn't yet know what he wants to do with his life. At twenty two years of age it is maybe not that surprising.

Sarah has been our Saturday explosion for two years. She came to me pleading that I just had to employ her because she was so right for the job, and that the shop couldn't possibly do without her. Somehow she convinced me, and she certainly does liven up a

Saturday morning. She is probably in her early twenties, and it was rumoured at one time that she had a crush on me. Whether this was true or not I shall probably never know, never having encouraged her, or ever been attracted to her. Other staff come and go, and there are various 'backups' I can call upon at particularly busy times, or if someone is off sick. All in all we are a good team, and the shop is very successful. I am considering opening up a second floor in the near future. It would mean employing more staff of course, but I hope it would pay for itself. I am putting the decision on hold until after the Christmas rush, and the post Christmas blues. If we can get through that with a substantial profit, then I see little more than planning permission getting in our way.

Mark brought over a strong black coffee; I was beginning to feel weary. It was by now the middle of the afternoon, and there had been no sign of Katie. Mark casually enquired whether I was OK. I don't think he was overly interested in my wellbeing, but thought he ought to ask. He had become used to me coming into work with the odd hangover, and knew how to keep out of my way. I was always very serious about the shop, and have never missed a day's work. I hardly ever took a lunch break either, and quite often stayed behind after closing time, sorting deliveries, stock-taking and generally keeping things in order.

It was obvious Mark respected me for my devotion and would never intentionally do anything that would upset me. However he was at times prone to 'putting his foot in it', and as a result had become very cautious when broaching delicate subjects. Yet he was naturally very curious, and sometimes just couldn't help himself. I told him I was fine, that I had just had a busy weekend, and that it was all catching up on me. He laughed and asked how Rachel was. I looked at him sternly, he shuffled his feet and announced he had some forms to attend to. I was actually beginning to miss Louise, her constant supply of caffeine, and her knack of keeping Mark in check when needed. Then she arrived, and I realised I didn't miss her at all, and that I had just gone through a momentary lapse of reality. It was all kisses and concerned chit-chat. I felt quite nauseous watching her and Mark greet each other as though one of them had just returned from a dangerous voyage at sea. Then, sure enough, not five minutes after her arrival, she approached me with a cup of coffee. It was much better than the one Mark had just given me, and I drank it in earnest.

Still no Katie. Maybe she wasn't going to show after all. Maybe that was it. A one night wonder. I started to feel depressed, what if I had really offended her? I may never see her again and be left with this longing, haunting me for the rest of my life.

I spent three days waiting and wondering whether she would come to see me, she didn't. It was getting to the point where I could hardly concentrate on things. I was becoming distracted at work, the flat was becoming even more neglected than usual. I decided to call on Niall's sensible advice.

Niall worked at a bank; it would not have been my choice, but he enjoyed it. He'd been working there for about eight years and had gained himself a very good position. He was comfortably off, owned a large two-bedroom flat in the centre of town, and a brand new car. I was put through to his extension.

"Niall, it's Jaz. Look I'm really sorry about Saturday night. The food was fantastic. I hope Susie wasn't too disappointed."

"She was OK. I think Rachel was the one most disappointed. Did you go the club? What happened?"

"I had the best night of my life, mate. But I could really do with some advice. Any chance we could meet up tonight?"

"Sorry mate, I'm going to Susie's tonight. Tell you what though, why don't you come round too?"

"I'm not sure, I wanted to talk to you alone."

"OK, I'll ring Susie and say I'll be a bit late. Shall we meet for a quick drink in The Ram, say about seven thirty? That'll give us time for a chat and I could be at Susie's for half eight."

"Cheers Niall, I really appreciate it." I felt a sense of relief that I could at least offload some of the turmoil on to someone else to figure out.

Chapter seven

I arrived at The Ram earlier than the arranged time, impatient to see Niall and get a second opinion. I somehow thought that if I arrived early I would see him sooner. Niall was ten minutes late.

"Hi Jaz, do you want a drink?"

"Thanks Niall, I'll have a pint."

We sat at a small round table with our drinks and cigarettes. The Ram was not a terribly exciting pub, especially at this time of night, in the middle of the week. It was a bit oldie worldie, but it was comfortable and warm, with its imitation coal fires, thick red carpets and velvet upholstery, which may have looked nice a few years ago, but were now in definite need of replacing. But it had a good juke box and decent beer on draught.

I told Niall all about my adventures with Katie. He listened with keen interest, laughing at some of the things I relayed to him, looking shocked at others and positively in awe at the rest. I finished my tale, awaiting a positive solution to my dilemma.

"Wow Jaz, she sounds wild. If I were you I would put it all down to experience, if you get together with her again, then enjoy. I wouldn't hold your breath though. It sounds to me as though that could well have been it. I'm afraid I think it's unlikely that you'll see her again. She obviously doesn't want a commitment, she's out for a laugh, mate, and I think the joke's been on you.

You'd be best off forgetting all about her and getting on with your own life. You've got too much going for you to waste your energy on someone who doesn't appreciate you. I mean, where would it go? There's also the child, where does she fit into the grand scheme of things?" Niall was telling me things I didn't want to hear. I wanted him to tell me she would be waiting around the corner for me. That I was going to have hundreds of nights like the one we'd already shared. Of course he was right, and I knew it.

Niall had to go and keep his date with Susie. I was left feeling deflated. I think I needed to hear what Niall had said, afterall he was only echoing my own fears. I had to be realistic, and besides wonderful things just don't happen to me. I was starting to pity myself and needed a distraction. I wondered what Rachel was up to tonight. I took out a Marlboro and lit it up. Next step, find a telephone.

"Rachel, it's Jaz. I wondered what you were doing tonight, could I come and see you?" Rachel wasn't the sort of person with whom I could just turn up and visit without arranging it first. I am not quite sure why, but she is very ordered, not at all impulsive. I think if I had just turned up unannounced, she would probably have a face pack on, or her hair in curlers. I may be being unfair, but I don't think so.

"Sure Jaz, come round, I've been wondering how you were."

Distraction arranged, I stopped by the off licence and bought a bottle of wine and some cigarettes, and made my way confidently to Rachel's. Rachel lived in a studio flat on the top floor of an old coach house. It was open plan and surprisingly spacious. It had large windows in the roof, one above her bed in the bedroom. I had always wanted to lie in her bed and look up at the night sky through it. Rachel opened the door looking as immaculate as ever.

"Come on in, don't let the cold in. Oh, you've bought some wine, I'll go and get some glasses." I sat down on one of her two cream-coloured sofas and looked at her cream coloured rug, and wondered how she kept it so clean. The whole flat was very tidy. Objects were placed in precise positions. Katie wouldn't have a flat like this, I thought to myself.

Rachel was wearing a dark, low neck cardigan and dark leggings. Somehow she always managed to have her ample cleavage exposed. She had dark bobbed hair and brown eyes. She brought the drinks over and sat down next to me on the sofa. She held herself in a slightly coy manner; I couldn't help feeling it was all for effect. She was a dreadful tease and, in my experience, that was as far as it went. Yet tonight I felt something different about her presence. I think maybe Niall had been right when he said that I now had Rachel exactly where I wanted her. Trouble was I didn't want her any more. The chase had gone on too long and burnt itself out. I suddenly felt that coming here had been a mistake. I didn't want Rachel to think I was still interested in sleeping with her.

"So, how are you feeling now, are you better?" she enquired. *Better?* I thought. *Had I been ill?* Then I remembered my abrupt exit from the dinner party.

"Yes, I'm much better, a day in bed soon cured me. How was the party after I left? Did it go on for long?"

"It was great, wasn't the food good?" This wasn't working. I couldn't stop wishing I was with Katie. I wanted to leave.

"I missed you, Jaz. Look I know I may've been a bit rotten to you lately, but it's only because I really like you." Was this supposed to make sense? I am sure I will never understand women. I wanted to stop her from saying any more, afraid of what might be to come. "You see, Jaz, I had to make sure you were the right one, before I gave myself to you. I had to test you," she continued. She made it sound as though she were a virgin entering into life long marriage. I had only wanted to have sex with her.

"What do you mean test me, Rachel? I only thought we could have great sex together, that was all. Nothing heavy."

"I know that now Jaz, and that's OK. But you see I had to work out whether it was OK or not." I was becoming more confused by the minute. "And I have decided it's OK."

Terrific and thank you very much Rachel for thinking that I am good enough for you. Why did it take you so long to figure it out? Was another of the more polite thoughts running around inside my brain. With that she took my glass out of my hand and pounced on me. Before I knew it she had taken her clothes off and was unbuttoning my fly. Needless to say I didn't put up much resistance, and we made love on her cream sofa.

I woke up to bright sunlight shining down on my face from the roof window. What had I done? What a terrible mistake. I felt cross with myself. I'd used Rachel and it wasn't fair on her. She didn't deserve it. I reached out for a cigarette. She woke up and smiled at me.

"Rachel..." I started to say.

"Yes, Jaz," she answered coyly. What was I to do? I couldn't tell her it had all been a mistake.

"Any chance of a coffee?"

"Sure," she replied. With that she got out of bed, put on a silk dressing gown and went to make the coffee. I got out of bed and dressed before she came back in.

"Oh, you're up," she said, surprised, as she brought the coffees in.

"Yeah, I have to go to the flat before opening up the shop."

I felt awkward and deceitful. I just wanted to leave as soon as possible.

"Oh, I see," was her somewhat distant reply. "Will I see you again?" I could tell by the way she said it that she already knew the answer.

"Look Rachel, I'm really sorry, really I am. I've just got a lot on my mind at the moment. It's not you, it's just bad timing. I enjoyed last night, really I did." I was trying to make the best of a bad job. Rachel was suitably unimpressed.

"Goodbye Jaz, I knew I should have trusted my instincts." With that she slammed the front door shut, tears falling down her cheeks.

I shuffled back to my flat smoking a cigarette. As I passed all the people on their way to work, smart clothes, briefcases and umbrellas in hands, afterall, you never know what the English weather may do, I wondered what they had all done last night. Had any of them hurt a friend's feelings, and if they had, how can they be walking along the street as though it were 'just another day'?

Chapter eight

Thursday dragged by very slowly. I tried to spend as much time as possible out at the back of the shop, sorting through deliveries and old stock. I couldn't face the public today. Mark had realised that things weren't quite right, Geoff was oblivious. Mark, bless him, always concerned, he meant well.

"Jaz, are you OK, only I've noticed that you've not been quite yourself lately? Louise tells me not to interfere, but you're a mate, and I don't like to see you this way. Is it girl trouble?"

My first instinct was to throw an empty cardboard box at him and tell him to get back to work and mind his own business. Then I thought that wasn't very fair, so decided to shock him instead.

"I had rampant sex with a total stranger for twenty-four hours while consuming large amounts of cocaine, then a few days later, blatantly used a good friend for her body alone, and will probably never see either of them again!" That did the trick.

"Oh, I see," was Mark's stunned reply. I turned around and got on with the sorting. Mark made a cautious retreat, not knowing quite what to do or say. Maybe it would have been kinder to just throw the box at him afterall.

Eventually the day was over, everyone had left. I got my coat, put my cigarettes and lighter in my pocket, and turned the power to the shop off. I walked out into the street and locked the door. Niall was waiting outside.

"I got a phone call from Susie at work, says she doesn't want to see me tonight. Something to do with my lousy choice of friends and that Rachel was going over in a state."

"This is really getting out of hand. Look I've fancied Rachel for ages everyone knows that. It's just not the same feeling as I have for Katie."

"Did you tell Rachel about Katie?"

"How could I? What is there to tell anyway. I'm really sorry I upset Rachel. The timing just wasn't right. Do you want to come back to my place, we can get some beers in and watch a video?"

"Sure, I've got nothing better to do, thanks to you."

We went back to my flat and had a really good evening, realising that we hadn't had a boy's night for ages. Niall left at a reasonable hour and I managed to get to bed relatively early and catch up on some much needed sleep. In the morning I felt much better. I got up, pulled my jeans on, lit up a cigarette and drew open the curtains in the living room. It was another beautiful sunny day, very crisp. The green was covered in a layer of white frost and I could see people scraping the ice off their car windscreens. Children were wrapped up in coats and hats making their way to school. I found the view out of my window very reassuring. It was always the same in principal, it was just the characters who changed. I had managed to convince myself that I hadn't done anything too terrible. That in fact, Rachel had been a more than willing participant. I had enjoyed having sex with her and I was pretty sure that she felt the same. It was bound to have happened at some time, and soon she would realise all this too and we could be friends again.

Guilt successfully eradicated, I finished my coffee. I got suitably dressed for the outside world, lit up a cigarette and walked into work. It was a typical start to the day and Mark and Louise seemed much relieved that I was back to my normal self. Geoff looked a bit rough this morning.

"Good night was it?" I asked teasing.

"Yeah, I went to this mega party, Sarah was there. It was in the grounds of a stately home. It was wild, there were fun fair rides, and two huge marquees with awesome sounds. Oh yeah, and I met one of your friends there, said to say hi." I couldn't think of any of my friends who would go to a party like that and not tell me beforehand.

"Who was that then?" Geoff had probably got mixed up, it was probably one of the customers. It wouldn't have been the first time a customer had claimed to be one of my friends.

"Can't remember her name, but wow she was something else, the way she danced and moved, I could've watched her all night. Anyhow I got chatting to her, told her I worked here and she says she knows you, said to say hi."

"What did she look like?" I asked, my heart racing. "Stunning! She had these gorgeous sexy eyes and smile. She had fair hair I think, it was tied back with a shoe lace, she was quite small. She was really good fun."

It was her, it had to be Katie. I felt overcome with jealousy, how well had Geoff got to know her. Why had I not been at the party instead of him?

"It sounds like Katie, did she say she'd pop in?"

"Katie, that was it. No, she didn't say she'd pop in."

With that Geoff went back to tidying shelves. I needed to know how close he had got to her, but I didn't know how to ask him.

Just then Katie walked in, pushing Freya in a buggy. She looked gorgeous. Her hair was still tied back, as Geoff had described it, with a shoe lace. She was wearing dark blue tatty Levi jeans, a black jumper and her hip length jacket. A moment of panic came over me. Had she come to see Geoff? Was I going to have to watch them being intimate with each other in front of my very eyes? She walked past Geoff, smiled at him, said what a great party it had been, and then proceeded to come over to me at the counter.

"Hiya," she said, smiling, looking at me with those eyes.

"Hi," I replied nervously. She'd come to see me. I didn't want to mess things up this time. I had to be careful.

"I thought I'd come and check out the shop, it's pretty cool. There's so much here. I can't believe I've not been here before," she said casting her eyes along the shelves.

"I'm glad you came. Here Freya, you can have one of these." I handed Freya a Spiderman rubber doll. We had a whole pile of them for sale on the side of the counter. Freya seemed pleased with her new toy. "Do you want to go somewhere for a drink?" I offered Katie.

"Love to, I could really do with a strong coffee. I went to a fab party last night."

"Yeah, I know, Geoff was just telling me about it." This statement didn't produce any reaction from Katie, so I felt reassured that Geoff's encounter had been purely innocent.

"Mark, I'm going out for a bit, can you hold the fort until I get back?" Mark looked completely stunned and just stared vacantly at me and Katie. Louise nudged Mark in the ribs. He suddenly came to life.

"Yes, sure, of course, why not." Louise nudged him again and he shut up. Maybe I should start paying Louise afterall.

I got my coat and cigarettes and Katie, Freya and I left the shop.

"Where do you want to go?" I asked.

"Anywhere warm," she replied, smiling. I wanted to put my arm around her, but didn't feel that I could. I remembered that there was a cafe which had a children's play area in, so we all went there. We settled down with our coffees, while Freya found some toys and friends to play with.

"Your shop's great." Katie said, offering me a cigarette. I didn't know what to say to her, terrified of saying the wrong thing.

"My shop's my baby," I replied, accepting the cigarette. "You should've come to the party, you'd have had a great time," she said softly.

"I didn't know about it," I answered.

We sat in silence for a few minutes. She was looking at me smiling with her eyes, the way she did. The silence didn't feel awkward, it was such a pleasure to be sitting with her, looking at her.

She didn't mention our night together, and neither did I. We simply drank our coffees, talked about nothing in particular, and eventually left. Katie pushed Freya in the buggy, and we walked along the street.

"I've got to get Freya back and give her lunch," she said, apologetically.

"Would it be OK if I came too?" I asked impulsively, not wanting to lose her again.

"Sure," she replied, smiling.

I felt bad about leaving the shop for so long, but this was really important. Besides, I rarely left the shop, I was due a break. We walked along the pavement together. It felt strange Freya being there too, almost like a family. As we walked along the street Katie stopped and chatted to various people. She seemed to know everyone.

We eventually came to a large slightly run-down looking house. Katie lifted up a stone from the windowsill and pulled out a front door key. She opened the large front door with its peeling paint, and replaced the key. We entered into the large hallway. It was filled with clutter. There were children's boots and coats lying on the floor, bicycles leaning against the walls, toys scattered around the place. Katie pushed the buggy into the hall, then unstrapped Freya, who climbed out and disappeared through one of the doors. The house felt cold and smelt slightly damp.

"Come on through," Katie beckoned and I followed her through one of the doors. We entered into a massive room with huge double doors opening into another room at the rear of the house. The room was just as chaotic as the hall, but it had a friendly atmosphere. It was filled with odd bits of antique furniture, old leather sofas covered with embroidered Indian cushions, Persian rugs covered the floor. Large dark green velvet curtains hung untidily in the windows. A big black marble fireplace had bits of paper, postcards, cigarette ends, Victorian vases and all sorts of strange objects piled on top of it. A huge gilt-framed mirror stood on top of the fireplace, most of the silver had worn off the back which made it look grey and black. There was a writing desk, at least three bookshelves and a dresser in the room, all covered with a strange mixture of books, children's toys, antique ornaments, CDs and mugs. The walls were covered with large-framed paintings. There was a fire burning in the grate. Katie put some more wood on.

"Hello, Katie," a woman's voice called from another room. The woman came in the room holding Freya's and another child's hands. "Hello," she said addressing me. "I'm Hetty." Hetty was older than Katie, I would say in her early thirties. She was tall and had very long, thick dark hair. She had a kind 'motherly' air about her and immediately made me feel welcome.

"How were the kids last night?" Katie asked.

"They were fine. George was making a bit of fuss, but Henry and Freya went to sleep like a log. Rebecca stayed up late as usual. Did you have a good time?"

"Yeah it was great. Hetty why don't you go out for the afternoon, I'll look after the kids and pick George and Rebecca up from school," Katie offered.

"OK, great. Simon will be back about six as usual, but I'll probably be back by then anyway. Do you know your plans for tonight?"

Katie laughed. "Do I ever?" she said.

"Well, you know where the key is if you want to crash here." With that Hetty kissed the children and left saying goodbye.

"So this is where you live?" I enquired cautiously.

"Sometimes," Katie replied. "It's Freya's home really, Hetty's great with the kids and I feel happy leaving her here."

"So Freya doesn't live with you?" I asked surprised. "I've got to make the kids some food. Do you want to come through to the kitchen?" Had I done it again? Had I asked too many personal questions? "You're really nosey aren't you?" she paused. "I can't cope with Freya all the time. I love her so much, but I just need my own space. I can't be trapped like a caged animal. I have to be able to live. It's not right, I know that, but I've tried, I've tried really hard to be a good mother, and it just didn't work out. I came to resent her, and at that point Hetty offered to look after Freya. She loves children, she's a fantastic mother, and she and Simon have got three of their own. Simon's great as well, he's really laid back and mellow. It gives me time away from Freya, so that every moment I spend with her is really special and fresh. She means the world to me and I just want her to be happy. I wish that I could look after her all the time, but I can't," she said lighting up a cigarette, "I haven't admitted that to many people, you know," she added hestitantly.

I felt very sorry for her. She had her head bowed and tears began to run down her face. There was a deep sadness and vulnerability surrounding Katie now. I came closer to her and put my arms around her. She sobbed into my chest. What had made her this way, why was motherhood so difficult for her? I had always believed it to be the most natural thing in the world.

I had to get back to the shop and I felt that Katie needed to be on her own with the children. I held her head up, gently wiped away the tears and kissed her on the lips.
"Can I see you tonight?" I asked.
"Do you want to?" she asked, surprised. I held her close to me again.
"You bet," I replied. "Come to my flat when you're ready and I'll take you out for a meal."
"OK." she replied, her face lighting up.

I wrote down my address and telephone number and gave it to her; she placed it in her back jean's pocket.

Chapter nine

I left the house feeling quite shocked at the things Katie had told me. I had little experience of children, so felt that I probably shouldn't make a judgement on a topic I knew very little about.

I had been gone from the shop for about four hours; this was bad news. I'd never been away for that length of time before. I almost ran back, fearing all sorts of disasters.

"Thank God you're back, Jaz. Things are getting pretty hectic here," said Mark in his 'Hello, welcome back, did you have a nice time?' sort of way. The shop was indeed very busy. It was the run up to Christmas, an important time for business, I shouldn't have left the shop. I hate to think how much stock has gone 'missing'. I apologised to everyone and was beginning to think that Katie wasn't a good influence on me.

"I think maybe it's time to call in one of the 'support staff'," I suggested. Mark agreed and I set about making some phone calls. After making several unsuccessful calls, I finally got hold of Johnny. Johnny was a self-employed illustrator. He illustrated mainly books and journals and had recently started to branch out into greeting cards. He was fairly successful, although always in need of extra cash. He could start tomorrow, Saturday.

Louise came over with one of her wonderful cups of coffee.

"Thanks, Louise. Louise, what do you know about children?" What possessed me to start a conversation with Louise, I don't know.

"Well, my sister's got two. What did you want to know?" replied Louise, obviously as surprised as I was that I had asked her.

"I don't know really. Do you think they need their mothers looking after them?"

"Well, I think so, yes. But then again, lots of mothers go out to work these days and leave their children with childminders, and lots have full-time nannies. Then you get some fathers who bring up the children."

I wished I hadn't asked, Louise was so unopinionated. She could always see at least five sides to an argument, and never really seemed dedicated to any.

"Was that any help?" I refrained from answering, and thanked her again for the coffee.

I left work late that night; it was seven-thirty before I reached home. I jumped into the bath and had a cigarette. I had a proper date with Katie tonight, I had to look my best. I finished in the bath, had a shave, and doused myself with some expensive after-shave. I dressed in my best jeans and jumper, put some music on, and opened a bottle of champagne. I had a whole box of champagne which my friend Nick had brought back from a trip to France last month. Tonight, I felt, justified a celebration. It was now eight-thirty; she would be arriving any minute now, I thought.

An hour went by and no sign of Katie. I started to feel anxious. What if she had phoned while I was at work to say she could not make it? I hadn't left the answer phone on, I rarely did, I usually forgot. I stood by the window looking out onto the green to see whether I could see her coming. It was very dark tonight and the sky was clear. I could see all the stars shining brightly. I could see the wishing star, should I make a wish? It probably won't come true, but then I have nothing to lose…

I stood by the window for another half an hour. I had drunk almost the whole bottle of champagne and was running dangerously low on cigarettes. The phone rang, it had to be her, I quickly rummaged around for the phone.

"Katie!" I said excitedly.

"Rachel," Oh no, I thought, not now.

"Who's Katie?"

"Rachel, how are you?"

"Jaz, can you come over I really need to talk to you about the other night?" She sounded upset. Just then the door bell rang.

"Hang on a sec, Rachel, I've just got to answer the door." I left the receiver on the floor and ran down the stairs. It was Katie, looking as radiant as ever. We kissed passionately on the doorstep, then came up to the flat. I explained that I was on the phone and told her to open another bottle of champagne.

"Rachel, look I'm busy tonight. Can I give you a call tomorrow?"

"Who's there, Jaz, who's Katie?" Katie came in with the bottle and sat down opposite me, smiling, sipping her glass of champagne.

"Rachel, it's just a friend. I've got to go."

"You've got a girl there haven't you, bastard!" and with that Rachel hung up.

"Problems?" Katie asked smiling, knowingly. I took out a cigarette and lit it up.

"Just a friend, something happened that shouldn't have, and now she hates me."

"I find it hard to believe that anyone hates you, Jaz. She'll come round. When did this 'accident' happen?" she asked.

"Recently," was as honest as I could be.

"Give her time, she'll be fine."

"You don't know Rachel."

"No, but if she's a true friend she will," was Katie's calm, reassuring, reply.

"Katie, I slept with Rachel only a few days ago. My heart wasn't in it, it was with you."

"Hey, don't lay your guilt on me. I had nothing to do with it. You're the only one responsible for your actions. She's a friend, why shouldn't you sleep with her? It's only natural to be close to your friends."

"But Katie, I had only slept with you a few days before. Aren't you cross?"

"Why should I be cross? I slept with you because I wanted to. I don't own you. You don't own me. I sleep with lots of my friends, it's just another way of getting close."

"Have you slept with anyone since last weekend?" I asked, not really wanting to know the answer, but needing to.

"That's none of your business. Now stop getting heavy and let's have some fun. Here open your mouth and stick your tongue out." She placed what looked like a small piece of blotting paper onto my tongue, closed my mouth, smiled, and kissed me. Then placed one in her mouth too. My body started to tingle and I felt relaxed and calm. "Let's go to the fair," Katie said, excitedly, and jumped up in the air. I hated fairs, they were loud and expensive, but if that is was she wanted to do, then that was fine by me.

As we approached the funfair I could see all the bright lights, they seemed to be shimmering, and every colour seemed intensified. I could hear the music almost engulf me and go through my whole body. The fair was pulling us towards it, we couldn't get there fast enough and before I realised what was happening we were holding hands and running towards it. It felt so exciting, I wanted to go on every ride at the same time. We came to the huge Ferris wheel. We got into our seats, cuddling each other and feeling such an intense feeling of warmth and comfort, it almost felt as though we were wrapped up in a goose-feather duvet.

The wheel started to go up, and as we climbed higher into the night sky the fair grew smaller and smaller. We could now see over the whole city, all the street lights and Christmas lights were glowing. It all seemed very magical and unreal. Our seat was gently swaying as the wheel went around. We were now starting to descend back into the fair and the pulsating music. I could hear people's voices, but they didn't sound like voices, they sounded like a chattering, chanting sound. Round and round we went, it seemed like hours. Nothing seemed to matter, or even exist except Katie and I cuddled together as one.

Next ride was the Helter Skelter. Katie and I got our mats and chased each other to the top of the stairs. Katie got to the top first, she sat on her mat and went down the slide, I followed quickly behind trying to catch her up. I reached the bottom shortly after her and slid under her legs as she was standing up, she fell backwards and landed on top of me. We kissed, then she quickly jumped up and ran up the stairs again, I chased after her, both laughing uncontrollably. I caught up with her and this time we went down together on the same mat. Up and down we went, around and around the slide, until we had had enough and neither of us could stand up any more. We needed to find somewhere quiet to pause for a few minutes. We found a patch of grass and lay down on our backs looking up at the stars, which were shimmering and pulsating against an electric blue night sky, and caught our breath.

"I've never met anyone like you Katie. I think I'm falling in love with you." Katie laughed, and turned on her side, leaning over me, she kissed me.
"Don't be silly, that's the drug talking," and she lay back again on the grass, eyes staring at the sky. She

looked exsquisite.   I didn't have the energy or inclination at that moment to argue with her.   Though I think I really had fallen in love with her. "Let's go on another ride," she suggested.

I have no idea how long we were at the fair for, we must have gone on virtually every ride there was, at least twice, and every one as fun and as intense as the last. Every ride was a new and exciting experience. I dread to think how much money the fair made out of us, but it was worth it, nothing really seemed important except Katie and me in our own little 'bubble'. I never realised the fair, or drugs for that matter, could be so much fun.

The fair was starting to shut down and it was time to leave, we bought some drinks and some pink candy floss on the way out. Every time I tried to eat some of the candy floss it tickled my face and I ended up laughing, which made it impossible to actually eat any of it. Katie's candy floss looked as though it were attacking her face, it had got everywhere, in her hair, on her checks, her eyelashes, her clothes. Then she grabbed hold of what was left of it and threw it at me. Two can play at that game. I grabbed handfuls of my candy floss and started throwing it back at her. So started our candy floss fight. She chased me and when she caught up with me, she stuffed some down my back, laughing. Then she ran on ahead and I chased her and threw some at her hair. We played this game all the way back to my flat.

When we finally arrived we were both completely covered with bits of sticky pink candy floss and laughing so much I was losing my breath.

"I'm sticky." Katie said, laughing.

"Me too, I think a bath would be a good idea. Would you care to join me?" Katie agreed and we entered the house and climbed the stairs to my flat, my legs feeling tingly and jelly-like. I unlocked the front door and we tumbled inside. Katie went through to the living room and put on a CD. I went straight to the bathroom and turned on the bath water. Katie followed me in and started undressing me. I turned and, facing her, started to undress her too.

The bathroom was by now full of steam and we were completely naked. Katie reached for some bubble bath and began to empty about a quarter of the bottle into the water. As the water poured into the bath the bubbles grew and grew until they were flowing over sides of the bath and covering the floor.

I went through to the kitchen and collected some candles, a bottle of champagne and two glasses. I placed the candles around the sides of the bath and lit them, turned off the light and opened the bottle of champagne. We both climbed into the steaming hot bath water and I poured out a glass of champagne each. We sat facing each other at opposite ends of the bath, each holding a glass, and a cigarette. We were completely covered up to our chins in huge, frothing bubbles, each and every one containing all the bright colours of the rainbow. We had only the soft warm glow of candlelight to illuminate us. It was exquisite.

Chapter ten

The alarm clock pierced through my few remaining brain cells at eight a.m. It was Saturday morning, I think. I looked over in the bed next to me at the vision of loveliness that was Katie. There she lay peacefully asleep, I carefully removed some of her hair that had fallen over her face and kissed her gently on the cheek. I got up quietly so as not to wake her, went through to the living room and drew open the curtains. It was a misty November morning and it still had an air of surreal magic about it.

I lit up a cigarette and made some strong black coffee. I don't know what time we finally got to bed last night, but was sure it couldn't have been before four in the morning. I sat down on the sofa in the living room with my coffee and cigarette reflecting on the previous night. I couldn't remember having had so much fun in a long time. Katie was one special girl, but I knew that she wasn't mine, not yet anyway.

I had to get to work, although all I really wanted to do was get back into bed with Katie and spend the day with her. I wrote her a note, telling her I had left for work and to help herself to some coffee, and I asked her to drop into the shop later, if she could. I crept quietly out of the flat, feeling as though I had left most of myself still in the bed. I picked up the post from my letterbox on the way out, just a couple of bills that went straight into my coat pocket unopened. As I walked through the mist on the way to work, all my senses seemed to be heightened. Noises seemed very loud and clear, visually also, things appeared very precise.

I arrived at work a few minutes early, even so, everyone except Sarah and Johnny were already there.
"Good morning, everyone," I said happily. Everyone else just grumbled. Shortly afterwards Johnny arrived followed closely by Sarah, who was wearing a long length of tinsel wrapped around her neck and a pair of Christmas baubles hanging from her ears.
"Hello Jaz, I've brought some Christmas decorations in," she said enthusiastically, holding up a carrier bag full of tinsel and God knows what else. "I thought we could decorate the shop," she continued.
"Fine, go ahead," I replied in complete disbelief and resignation. I had come to realise that however hard I tried, no-one was going to let me believe that Christmas was at the end of December, that it was, in fact, in the middle of November.

"I saw you with Katie at The Dome last week," Sarah said.
"Do you know her?" I asked casually.
"Everyone knows Katie. She's a great girl, a lot of fun, but she's not good enough for you. She'll use you and she'll mess up your mind. She'll be a great friend, but don't get involved with her," she studied my expression and continued. "I can see by the look on your face that my advice is too late, you're bewitched."

Why was everyone so interested in my private life, and was Sarah ever going to come down to earth and stop believing in fairies, witches and Father Christmas?

"As it happens, Sarah, Katie and I are very close, and she is at this moment lying asleep in my bed."

"Of course she is. Just don't say I didn't warn you."

"Thanks for the warning, Sarah. Now go and dangle some tinsel, or maybe you don't want to work here anymore."

I felt cross, cross that my life didn't seem private, cross that I had raised to Sarah's bait and told her that Katie was at my flat. I was cross too because I was scared, scared that Sarah might be right. Too many people had warned me about becoming involved with Katie, but I was involved and I wouldn't have wanted it any other way.

That morning was very busy. Even with Johnny helping out we could probably still have done with an extra person. Louise was actually being very helpful and offered to help stack shelves. This put me in a bit of a dilemma, for if Louise was doing real work I would surely have to pay her. I decided I would let her chose something from the shop which she could take home. She thanked me about a hundred times, telling me in painful detail how she had her eye on a Judge Dredd annual for ages, but never been able to afford to buy it, and how kind I was. I instantly regretted my offer and vowed never to let Louise do any work in the shop again, however desperate I was.

I decided to phone home to see if Katie was up yet. There was no answer. Maybe she was still asleep, or maybe she was on her way to the shop. As soon as I put the receiver down, the phone rang.

"Hi Jaz, Niall here, are you very busy today?"

"Hello Niall, great to speak to you. Yes I am really busy, what can I do for you?"

"Oh, I was just ringing to see if there were any developments with Katie?"

"Yes, I spent last night with her, she is something else. She makes me feel so alive, I think I'm falling for her Niall."

"Well, when am I'm going to meet this bombshell?"

"Soon I hope. You and Susie friends again?" I asked.

"Yes, but then you know Susie and me, always breaking up and making up."

Susie and Niall did indeed have a volatile relationship, but I think they would get bored of each other if they didn't have so many arguments. It was obvious they were devoted, but they seemed to thrive on breaking up and making up. Not that their arguments were ever very serious and certainly not violent. It was difficult on their friends though, who were never quite sure of the current situation.

"I'll arrange something with Katie. We could all go out for a drink," I suggested.

The rest of the day was pretty uneventful. Very busy and good business though, but no sign of Katie. A few friends dropped by the shop during the day. Friends usually did drop in on Saturday, being as it was the only day they weren't at work, and the only place they were sure to find me. I hadn't told many people about Katie yet, I was still not quite sure where I stood with her. It was frustrating when friends did come into the shop, because I was never able to talk to them properly, always having to deal with the customers, especially on a busy day like today.

I was eager to get home at the end of the day to see if there was any sign of Katie, so I closed up the shop at six. As I locked the door I peered in through the window in shock at all the Christmas decorations taking over the ceiling and walls; I hadn't noticed them earlier, being so busy, but now they seemed to leap out and attack me. Maybe Sarah wouldn't notice if I took them down again.
I lit a cigarette and made my way quickly back to the flat.

As I crossed the green and approached my flat I looked up at the windows, in the vague hope there may be a light on. There wasn't. The curtains were still open and there was no sign of life inside. I reached the outside door and put my key in the keyhole and unlocked the door. The communal hallway was large and quite grand. It was painted magnolia, a colour I have always thought that people paint walls when they can't think of the right colour to suit a room; a sort of last resort, a safe bet. Why people paint a hallway a light colour was beyond me, I mean it gets so dirty, with people coming in and out all the time. Anyhow this is all rather academic seeing as I don't own my flat and am therefore not responsible for contributing to the upkeep of any part of the house.

I climbed the stairs feeling weary, it had been a long day and a long night. I opened my front door and switched the lights on. What a mess the flat was, I looked around for any sign of Katie, there was none, not even a note. Everything was as I had left it this morning, minus Katie lying in the bed. I wasn't really surprised. I was hungry, but couldn't face cooking, so I dialled a pizza. When it arrived I sat down infront of the television and ate. Body refuelled I climbed into bed, read a book and went to sleep. I'd sort out the flat in the morning.

Chapter eleven

I woke up and reached over to the clock, it was ten thirty in the morning. I felt refreshed from a good night's sleep. I went through to the living room opened the curtains and made the coffee. I sat down on the sofa, cigarette and coffee cup in hand and contemplated the day ahead. First priority was to clean the flat, after that I thought I might take the bike out for a raz and visit Jim and Liam. Jim had come into the shop yesterday and invited me over to his and Liam's place today. Jim and Liam live in a cottage on the outskirts of a village, about ten miles from the city. It is a beautiful place in the middle of nowhere, a real country retreat.

I met Jim through our mutual obsession with comics, he is in fact Trudie's brother. It was through Jim that I met and had a brief relationship with Trudie. Trudie has now moved on to another town and I rarely see her these days, but I keep in touch with Jim. Liam is Jim's lodger and a nice enough guy.

So that was my day sorted. I felt that if I filled my day up enough it would distract me from thinking about Katie, and hoping that she might get in touch. I managed to get the flat cleaned to a reasonable degree by midday, I had hoovered and made lots of new piles of comics, and put all the mugs and ashtrays I could find in the kitchen to be washed up later.

The weather was reasonable, it was cold and grey, but wasn't raining. I felt in the perfect mood to take the bike out. It wasn't often I got the chance to ride the bike properly, and I was looking forward to speeding along empty country lanes. I kept it in a shed at the back of the house, my 900cc Ducati.

I put on my leathers and helmet and started up the engine. Off I went; I had to go through a lot of the city before I could get out onto the dual carriageway which led out to Jim's village. The traffic was terrible, why were there so many cars on the road on a Sunday? I enjoyed riding through the centre of town, weaving in and out of the cars, watching them all standing still in their traffic jams, while I just cruised past them. It made me feel superior, momentarily. I also enjoyed the skill I had to use in controlling this immensely heavy machine at relatively low speeds, while at the same time negotiating the traffic ahead, and the lunatic car driver that inevitably pulls out without looking first, narrowly missing the bike and a potential accident.

I had reached the dual carriageway and now I could really open her up. I made good time and reached Jim's at one thirty. Jim opened the door and offered me a plate of left over lunch, which I gratefully accepted. I sat down in their small oak-beamed living room with the plate of food on my lap. This is what Sundays are about. Dan and Mike were there too and everyone was eating, drinking and reading the Sunday papers. The open fire was roaring and the whole place smelt strongly of wood smoke.

"So, what have you been up to Jaz? How's business, and what do you think of the latest 2000AD, pretty good, eh?" Jim asked. So conversation flowed throughout the afternoon, mainly on the topic of comics. It was starting to get dark and I thought it best to start making my way back to town. I had had a relaxing and distracting afternoon, just the tonic I needed.

I had enjoyed Jim's company, he was indeed a soulmate and he somehow always made me feel that everything was alright. He also had a bike which he rode every day into the city for work, but he loved the country and would find the city too claustrophobic to live in.

I started back on my journey home. It was now bitterly cold and starting to get icy, which made riding the bike tiring. When I reached town it was dark and there was still loads of traffic about, and people. There were lots of shops open too. It was all quite a culture shock, having spent an afternoon in the quiet green countryside, to be exposed to this neon nightmare. I thought about dropping by on Katie, would she mind? Would she even be there, Hetty's wasn't her house after all? Well I had nothing to lose. So it was a quick detour to see Katie. I pulled up outside. The lights were on which was promising. I turned off the engine, put the bike rest down and got off. Taking off my helmet and gloves I knocked on the door. Hetty answered.
"Hello," I said. "I wondered if Katie was in? I met you the other day, my name's Jaz."

"Hello, no I haven't seen Katie for a few days, sorry," was Hetty's disappointing reply.

A few days, I thought, so where was she last night? I was feeling confused and frustrated, but more than that, I felt a fool. I shouldn't have called on her, I've blown my cool. From now on I was going to play it super cool, if Katie wanted me, she was going to have to come and find me.

I put on my helmet and gloves and started the bike up. I got to the end of the road and stopped at the junction. I heard a familiar voice laughing, I turned my head towards the sound and there was Katie laughing, and in the arms of a slightly taller man who was also laughing. I could just make out in the dark who the man was. It was Miles, the guy in the cafe. They were staggering along the street together. She hadn't seen me, luckily. I rode off quickly before she noticed me. I felt cross and betrayed. I decided to go and see Niall. When I arrived at Niall's there was no reply, he must be at Susie's I thought. I rode the bike around to Susie's and rang on the doorbell. Susie answered.

"Susie, is Niall here? I've got to talk to him," I said abruptly. She said he was and asked me in, slightly bemused at my attitude. I walked into the living room, Niall was there, so was Rachel. I felt so angry that I didn't really care about Rachel's presence.

"Would you like some mulled wine?" Susie offered hesitantly, I accepted.

"Hello Jaz, you look in a bit of a state, what's up?" Niall asked.

"Katie is what's up. I just went to visit her, after not seeing her since I left her in bed yesterday morning, and she was in the arms of another man."

"Oh dear," was Niall's response, as he cautiously glanced at Rachel. Rachel didn't say a word, she just stared at me. I put my head in my hands and said out loud,

"Oh, what a mess, why did I ever get involved with her? Now I am involved with her, all I want is to be with her. I can't help it. She's such fun."

"Lucky girl," said Rachel coolly. I just looked at her in distaste, not in the mood to be sensitive to her feelings right now.

"So, tell me about Katie," said Susie calmly.

"She is just the most amazing person I've ever met."

"Does she think the same about you though? I don't know, but it seems to me that if she's with another bloke, that maybe her feelings aren't as strong as yours," Susie suggested.

"Well, I suppose she may not have been 'with' him, but they are good friends I know that much. I could have just misinterpreted the situation."

"What's her surname, it's not Crowe is it?" Susie asked.

"I don't know her surname," I replied.

"I used to know a Katie Crowe, used to go to the pub I used to go to, 'The Castle and Moat', or 'The Paddle and Float' as we used to call it. This was going back quite a few years, but she was wild. She had fair hair which was always a real mess, but she was really pretty. She had guys literally falling over themselves to chat her up. She was a real party animal, always with a different guy. I couldn't understand why they liked her so much. I mean she was very pretty, but not very 'ladylike'. She didn't wear make-up, or dress particularly well. She was a bit like 'one of the lads' really. Always drank pints, as much as any man, played football, rode motorbikes, smoked like a chimney and was really into drugs. She didn't give a damn what people thought of her and always hung around men. She had a couple of female friends, but always seemed a bit of a loner, like she didn't need to have loads of girlfriends around her all the time. Rumour had it she had a child, I hate to think what happened to her," Susie said.

"I'll tell you what happened to her, she met a really nice guy called Jaz, who fell in love with her. Susie that is the same Katie, it has to be. You said you couldn't understand the attraction, well I'll tell you what is it. It's for all the reasons you said. Because she is herself, she doesn't need to dress to impress, she does that with her warm and fun personality, and she doesn't need to wear make up because she is beautiful without it, plus I doubt whether she even thinks about what she looks like. And she probably spends more time with men, because they don't gossip and make judgements about people all the time."
"Steady on Jaz," Niall piped up.
"Blimey Jaz, you've got it bad," Rachel spoke for the first time.
"I'm sorry, but I really like her, and I don't know what to do about it," I said softly, looking at the ground.
"A distraction didn't even work did it?" Rachel said calmly. I looked up at her in a way as to say sorry, but

I couldn't answer her with words. She smiled at me, were we friends again?

I had spent so little time with Katie, but she sure had had an impact on me. I was like a fish on a hook, trying to wriggle free, but well and truly hooked. Niall suggested going away for a few days, but that was impossible, I had the shop to look after. No, I just had to carry on as usual and stop acting like an infatuated teenager.

Chapter twelve

Almost a week elapsed. It had been a busy week in the shop. We were now in the first week of December, it seemed as though everyone was doing their Christmas shopping very early this year. The shops were always full. We had been doing a roaring trade and have had Johnny working with us full time. Apart from work though, the week has been pretty static. I've been going to The Ram a lot after work with Niall, who has been making a concerted effort to try and distract me from thinking about Katie. I haven't seen or heard of her for a week.

It was Saturday night. I persuaded Niall to go to The Dome, only out of interest of course, to show him how it has changed. We did ask the girls, but they didn't fancy it, and went to the pictures to see a costume drama instead. It was eight when Niall turned up.

"I've just left Susie and Rachel at the flicks, and I've bought a couple of beers round to drink before we go out," Niall said offering me a can. We opened up the cans and sat down with a couple of cigarettes and listened to a new CD Niall had just bought. I couldn't help wondering if she would be there, well I would just have to wait and see. I wanted Niall to meet her too, if she was there. I was interested to know what his opinion of her would be.

It was time to start heading down town to The Dome. There was a heaving queue outside. We joined the end of the queue, which was moving pretty slowly. It was pitch black tonight and very cold with a feint hint of rain, but being in the queue huddled next to all the people we soon warmed up. A strutting figure came along the outside of the queue, it was Miles. He saw me and came over to Niall and myself with a big grin on his face.

"Hi mate! How's it going? Do you want to buy some whiz?" I gave him a negative reply, he then asked me if I had a spare cigarette I could give him. I gave him one and he lit it up. "So what have you been up to, mate?" he continued.

"Working," I replied, I didn't want to enter into a conversation with Miles, and resisted the temptation to just turn around and leave; instead I asked him if he had seen much of Katie lately.

"Sure, I see Katie all the time. Why, are you looking for her?" he replied.

"No, I just haven't seen her for a while that's all. I wondered how she was."

"Well you know Katie, she's always fine, she's probably around here somewhere." With that Miles strutted off to hassle some other clubgoers.

"Who was that?" Niall asked.

"That was Miles, the guy I saw Katie with last week."

"Really!" said Niall looking surprised, and stuck his head out of the crowd to get a good look at him.

We finally got inside the club, having waited about twenty minutes outside. The music was pounding, the air was full of smoke and the whole place was jam packed full of people. The atmosphere was lively and fun.

Niall and I made our way to the bar and after lots of pushing and shoving, finally managed to get to the bar and be served. It was then a matter of getting away from the bar with drinks unspilt, not an easy task when everybody else is pushing in the opposite direction, and not at all concerned that we had our full and paid for drinks in our hands. We finally got away, moderately unscathed having lost approximately a centimetre off the level of our beer.

"Maybe we should have bought two pints each. I don't fancy doing that again in a hurry!" Niall suggested practically.

We walked around the various rooms trying to find a seat, unsuccessfully, so we made our way to the dance floor where we could stand by the side and people watch. Niall was impressed with The Dome and was obviously enjoying the atmosphere.

"I can't believe the change in this place, and all these people, who are all these people? There's hardly anyone here I recognise. The music's great, Susie would love it down here!" Niall shouted over the music at me. There was no doubt about it, the place had a good vibe about it tonight and it was exciting; I felt that just about anything could happen. I tried to look through the crowds to see if I could catch a glimpse of Katie, but no luck yet.

Just then a couple of young girls, probably in their late teens came up to us and started chatting. One was much chattier than the other, who seemed quite quiet and stood behind her friend. The chatty one obviously fancied Niall, and was very drunk. Niall was quite charming to her for a while, until she tried to take a drink from his glass and drag him on to the dance floor. At which point Niall said, in his considerate subtle way, that they ought to be in bed by now with their teddy bears. This didn't go down too well and he discovered just how varied their swearing vocabulary was. I congratulated him on a job badly done and we moved to a different part of the room.

A track came on then that I recognised as the one Katie really liked, if she was here she would be dancing now. Sure enough I saw her. I watched her intently, in fact I couldn't take my eyes off her. She looked beautiful. She was wearing a short black dress, nothing dressy, just plain and simple, but she looked stunning. The way she moved to the music was hypnotic. She was completely in her own world, totally unaware of anything around her.

"There she is, Niall, there's Katie!" I pointed her out to him.

"Wow, I can see the attraction, how does she move like that? That's incredible. Are you going to call her over?"

"No, not yet. Let's just see if she sees me or not."

We watched her dancing to song after song, transfixed, we didn't even drink our drinks or smoke our cigarettes. Then a girl came up to her, who I hadn't seen before, and they started chatting, and eventually left the dance area together. I saw some money changing hands and then Katie disappeared out of the room, leaving the other girl standing leaning against the wall.

I then saw Miles come up to the girl, he had a joint in his hand which he passed to her. Just then these two huge guys appeared out of nowhere and started hitting Miles. The girl tried to move out of the way, but not quickly enough and got punched in the face. A punch that was destined for Miles, but which he had managed to duck out of. The next thing I knew Miles had disappeared, the girl was on the floor in tears, and the guys were standing there looking around for Miles.

Suddenly Katie reappeared, saw her friend on the floor and the two guys standing there. Without hesitation she gave one of the guys a punch in the stomach, and kicked the other one in the groin. Enough was enough, I wasn't going to stand here and watch Katie get pulverised by a couple of thugs and not do anything. I ran over to where all the commotion was going on and got there just in time to stop one of them from grabbing a hold of Katie. Niall quickly followed. The two guys looked at us.

"We have no argument with you?" they said.

"You just hit a woman, so we have an argument with you!" I said back to them. With that they turned and walked aggressively away.

Katie was leaning over her friend, I bent down to the floor. The girls face was bleeding and she was visibly shaken. Niall and I lifted her up and took her through to a room with some seats and sat her down. Katie followed us through.

"Candice, are you OK. What the hell happened?" Katie said to her friend, giving her a drink.

"Yeah, I'm OK. My face really hurts, those bastards, they were after Miles," Candice replied. Candice was of a similar build to Katie, with very classical looks, pale skin and long, fine, deep, dark red hair, probably hennaed.

"Was Miles OK?" Katie asked, concerned.

"Miles legged it didn't he, they didn't even get close," Candice answered in obvious pain.

"Do you feel faint?" Niall asked. She said she felt OK, just a bit shaken, and thanked us for helping her.

I sensed an attraction between Niall and Candice, but then all the girls fancied Niall. Niall had very blonde hair, almost white, which was short but with a fringe. He also had blue eyes, a large jaw and a stocky build, and was of a similar height to myself. He resembled a clean-cut Australian surfer. He was good looking, and he knew it. He had never had a problem getting a girl in his life. This inevitably created problems within his relationships. Susie was always accusing Niall of being a flirt, but poor Niall, he just couldn't help the fact that girls liked him. I don't think he is a flirt, on the whole he was happy with Susie and had no need to flirt.

It wasn't until now that Katie really acknowledged me. "Are you OK?" I asked her.

"Yeah, I'm fine. Who's your friend?" she asked.

"Katie meet Niall." Niall said hello, and Katie smiled at him. She then turned to me.

"It's really good to see you," she said smiling at me, and kissed me softly on the cheek. Katie then slipped a small package to Candice, she dipped her little finger into the powder and put it on her tongue.

"Not bad," Candice said.

"Only the best, of course," laughed Katie. "Hey there's a party tonight, do you guys want to come?" Katie asked us, enthusiastactly.

"Yeah, come along." entreated Candice. Niall and I looked at each other and nodded.

"Come on then, Candice has got a car," said Katie. With that we all got up and left the club and walked down the road to Candice's car.

Candice wasn't in a good way, she could hardly walk and her face hurt.

"I think we had better get a taxi," Niall suggested.

"OK, but lets go to the car first and cut this coke, I've got a mirror in there somewhere," Candice said. We got to the car, a battered old blue Chevette, which looked as though it had spent most of its life on a farmyard judging by the amount of mud and rust on it.

We all piled inside. Katie put a cassette on and Candice sorted out the cocaine, meanwhile I handed around the Marlboros. Niall, Candice and myself were huddled on the back of the car and Katie was in the front looking through the tapes. She pulled one out.

"Do you mind if I put this one on instead?" Katie asked holding a battered cassette up.

"That was Reuben's favourite," Candice answered thoughtfully.

"I know, that's why I wanted to put it on," Katie replied. Candice agreed.

"Who's Reuben?" Niall asked in his straight to the point manner.

"Reuben was Candice's lover, they had been inseparable for five years. He was also one of my best friends. He died about six months ago, he got busted by the police, he had a whole load of Ecstasy on him and he swallowed the lot. Within a few hours he was dead."

"I'm sorry, I shouldn't have asked," Niall said hurriedly.

"It's OK, it's good to talk about him," Candice said. With that Candice snorted a line of coke and passed around the mirror with the remaining three lines on it, Niall was very reticent about the cocaine and refused to partake in the consumption of illicit substances. "I think about him all the time, he's always with me, so why not talk about him? He had so many friends that if we didn't talk about him, nobody would be speaking to each other!" said Candice, laughing.

"I've never known anyone die, except my grandfather, and that was a real shock," Niall said.

"I know so many people who've died one way or another, I've lost count. I just think that wherever they all are right now, there must be one of the best parties going on," laughed Katie.

"Talking about parties, are we going to get a cab or what?" Candice said.

Katie turned the music off, Candice put the remaining cocaine in her pocket and we all got out of the car.

Chapter thirteen

The party was in a squat in a large run-down house. The staircase was huge, and covered with bodies, some unconscious, some kissing, others just groups of people smoking joints, drinking, chatting and laughing. There were loads of rooms, they all seemed to be packed. The music was very loud, it was good music and in one of the rooms a live band were playing. There was very little furniture, just lots of old mattresses covering the floors, and a few old chairs and tables here and there. There were different coloured light bulbs in each room. The floors were littered with empty cans and bottles. The party had obviously been going for some time before we got there, but it was still going strong.

Katie and Candice seemed to know just about everyone there, and it wasn't long before we each had a bottle in our hands, sitting around a table, Candice cutting some more lines of cocaine and Katie rolling a joint. Niall was having a good time and so was I, but I wanted to hold Katie and be alone with her so much. The room we were in was full of people, one guy came over to Katie and crouched down next to her. I couldn't hear what he was saying, but she was laughing. The next thing I saw he had his arms around her waist and they were kissing passionately. Niall looked at me, and I looked back at him. That was it, I was off. I stood up and walked out of the room, pushing people out of my way. Niall shouted after me, but I just kept on going. I got to the stairs and started hurriedly making my way down them.

"Jaz, stop, wait!" cried Katie leaning over the banister above me. I kept on going down the stairs as quickly as I could. I wanted to get away from her, fast. She kept calling to me to stop, and was running down after me. When I got to the bottom, I sat down and pulled my packet of Marlboro from my coat pocket, and lit one up. Katie came and sat next to me.

"Jaz, what's up?" she asked, looking worried and confused. I looked at her in disbelief. "Look Jaz, I don't know what you want from me. I thought we were friends," she said, bewildered.

"So did I!" I replied.

"So what's the problem?" she asked.

"You really don't get it do you? I really like you Katie. I have done since the moment I saw you in the park. I have been unable to stop thinking about you. I thought we had something going between us, now I just realise I've been made a fool of!" Katie didn't answer, she just sat there, smoking a cigarette, looking sadly into space.

"Well?" I demanded.

"Well," said Katie hesitantly, "I really like you too, a lot, and it really scares me," she paused. "I'm not into relationships and all that emotional baggage. I like having fun with guys, it's a laugh, you know, we're mates and sometimes we end up in bed, sometimes we don't, it doesn't mean anything, it's no big deal. Sometimes guys do really fall for me and they get hurt, but on the whole that's their lookout. I never promised anyone anything, I'm not responsible for their fragile emotions. Unfortunately though, it means sometimes, I lose their friendships, which makes me sad. But on the whole there isn't a problem, and I have a lot of really good mates whom I love to bits."

"So you don't give a damn about people's feelings then. You don't care about guys like me getting hurt, because you're not responsible, even though you allowed them to get close to you in the first place," I retorted angrily. "But it's different with you, Jaz. I don't know, it just feels different with you, I really like you, more than I can say. I haven't felt like this about a guy since Freya's dad, and it really scares me. I don't know how to handle you, so I try to keep away from you. That way if I don't see you, maybe I can forget about you, and we won't end up hurting each other. But that's easier said than done."

I took Katie in my arms, and we kissed. I couldn't be cross with her because I really think that she doesn't mean to hurt intentionally, I just don't think she realises the effect she has on men, and besides I was in love with her. She sat astride me on the stairs, and put her hands under my t-shirt and was stroking my skin. I had my hands on her thighs, gently caressing her, and slowly moving my hands further up her dress. We sat like that for a few minutes, passionately kissing and fondling each other. Then she slowly got up, held my hand and led me into a small dark empty room on the ground floor, where we lay down on a bare mattress and made love.

We lay there in the dark smoking our post-coital Marlboros. Most times when I have made love to a woman, I have a strong desire to immediately go into deep satisfied sleep, or to get up and get on with doing something constructive. But not when I'm with Katie. When I have made love to Katie I just want to lie as close to her as I can, to hold her in my arms and kiss her all over, and then do it all again as soon as possible.

There were no curtains on the huge windows of the room and a few of the glass panes were broken. The orange glow of street lights flickered into the room, creating large shadows as the trees moved in the wind. I could hear the rain tapping on the glass, the odd car drive past, and the muffled sound of people's voices in the street outside. The heavy door to the room was shut, so all I could hear from the party was the pounding bass of the music, and people shouting on the stairs.

We lay on the mattress naked, with only my large coat covering us, she had her head on my shoulder, I had my arm around her. We didn't speak. I felt I could lie like this forever, in our own peaceful, content, cocoon, away from all the noise and hustle.

Our paradise was rudely interrupted but a group of youths who bounded their way into the room, believing it to be empty.
"Don't mind us," a young lad said when they realised we were in there, and proceeded to sit around in a huddle and light up a bong, ignoring us completely.

They had left the door wide open and it was not long before people started piling into the room. This proved to be too much for Katie, who suddenly stood up, completely naked, and started throwing clothes at everyone, yelling at them to piss off. The ones who hadn't responded to the clothes, she went up to and started kicking, with her bare feet, still completely naked. It really was hilarious to watch, these kids trying to gather their bits of dope, skins, cigarettes and matches together while being kicked out of the room by a small, irate naked woman.

Chapter fourteen

After Katie had managed to get everyone out of the room, she forced a chair under the door handle, making it impossible to open. She came back to 'bed', collecting a couple coats that had been left behind in the exodus, and put them on top of us. With the extra layers and our joint body heat, we were quite warm.

"Have another Marlboro," I offered.

"Have another line," Katie offered back, smiling. We proceeded to smoke more cigarettes, and snort more cocaine. I don't know if it was the effects of the coke, or just the magic of the moment, but I felt as though Katie might now actually open up about herself, if I dared to ask. I wanted to find out all about her, but she had always been so guarded. I decided to go for it.

"Katie," I said casually, "Have you lived in the city long?" To my astonishment she didn't jump up in a fit of indignant fury, spouting on about intrusion of privacy, as she had always done previously when I had started one of these conversations. Instead she inhaled deeply on her cigarette and began talking calmly.

"When I was sixteen there was this terrible scene at home, things had been pretty bad for as long as I can remember, but never that bad. I had enough, it was time to jump ship. I walked out of the house with nothing, leaving my two older brothers and my mother and father screaming at each other, I don't even think they noticed I had gone. All I knew was that I wanted to get as far away as possible.

I had a good friend, Bess, who had moved to the city recently to live with her older sister, I decided I'd look her up. It was about a hundred miles away, I had no money so I had to hitch. It took me a whole day and three rides to get here. One driver tried it on with me, so I told him to pull over 'so we could have some fun'. When he pulled over I grabbed hold of his testicles and squeezed them as hard as I could and ran off, luckily getting another lift immediately. My first lesson in survival," she giggled. "When I arrived in this city it was dark. I had Bess' address but had no idea how to get there. Eventually I found it, I was hungry and cold. Hetty, who is Bess' elder sister opened the door. Bess was so pleased to see me. They are such a warm happy family. They welcomed me in and made me some food. Hetty and Simon's house is massive, and they only had two children then so there was plenty of room for me to stay. Even so, I shared a room with Bess. They were wonderful, they didn't ask any awkward questions or make any judgements.

I lived with them for about a year. Bess and I were inseparable, we did everything together. We both worked as waitresses in a restaurant, which was fun. We earned so much money. I didn't pay Hetty rent, just money for food and bills; Bess did the same. So compared with most girls our age, we were rich and we had a ball. We both looked a lot older than we were and had no trouble getting into pubs and clubs and we made some brilliant friends. I think of my friends as my family now, we look out for each other and if any of us ever gets into a scrape, we all get together and help out in any way we can."

"Does Miles come into this category?" I interrupted. "Definitely, and Candice and Reuben, and a whole lot more. It was after I'd been here a year that I met Freya's father. He was so cool, I fell for him big time, and he was from this really wealthy family; he was loaded. We had a wild passionate affair, taking cocktails of drugs and partying all the time. I soon gave up the waitressing and moved in with him. He had this gorgeous flat that Mummy and Daddy had bought him; I was in heaven.

Shortly after I moved in I found out I was pregnant, I was really happy and so was he, I thought. Then one morning Hetty came around to the flat in a terrible state, when we had finally calmed her down she told us what was wrong. The night before Bess had been involved in a car accident. Dave, a good friend of ours, had been driving, Bess had been in the passenger seat. She had been killed instantly, Dave was still in hospital in intensive care. He made a full recovery luckily.

It was a terrible shock, the first person I had known to have died. It brought me and Hetty very close; I became the sister she lost. Everything seemed to go down hill from then on. Freya's dad started getting heavily into smack, which alienated me from him, because I was pregnant I had stopped taking drugs altogether. We were on a totally different wavelength and couldn't communicate at all.

Then his close friend Tom died of an accidental overdose. I thought Tom's death would make him stop taking smack, but he just got worse. He couldn't deal with his feelings and the heroin blocked them all out. His parents got wind of what was happening and started threatening to stop his money if he didn't pull himself together, and I think if it hadn't been for me being pregnant they would have done there and then. He was oblivious to any threats though; he'd left reality months ago." Katie paused and took a few drags of her cigarette.

She looked pained and sad, tears were welling up in her eyes. Then she smiled.
"Freya was born in the spring, she was so beautiful. The most precious thing in the world to me. Hetty and Simon took me home to the flat from hospital, as Freya's dad couldn't get it together to fetch me. I stayed with him for about a year after her birth, but it was hopeless. Hetty suggested Freya and I moved in with her until I got myself sorted out, so we did. Shortly after I left him, his parents disowned him and stopped all his money, he kept the flat and now gets his drugs on prescription. His parents have been really good to Freya though, and continue to give me money for her now. They now live in Switzerland, but see Freya as often as they can. They totally dote on her, which is sweet. They deposit some money into a bank account every month for her. It's not a silly amount, but enough

to help out with the necessities; I'd find things really difficult without it.

At first I got a flat for us both, their money covered the rent and the food, but I just couldn't cope with being a full-time mum. I felt so trapped and I tried for a long time to fight it, but I was fit to burst; I needed my freedom. Hetty saw the state I was in and suggested looking after Freya for a while. Their third child was about the same age, it would be good company for them both, so Freya moved in with Hetty. I kept my flat for a couple of months after that, but found that I was hardly ever there - I was always crashing at friend's places or at Hetty's - so I gave up the flat and gave some of the grandparents' money to Hetty instead, for looking after Freya. I needed money for myself, and although I was getting all the state benefits I was entitled to, it wasn't enough, so I started dealing. I had all the contacts already. I started off dealing just dope, but having developed a liking for cocaine, started dealing that too. I make enough to live on. I don't have a flat, so there's no rent or bills to pay. The money from Freya's grandparents pay for her needs, and the drugs pay for themselves. I'll be rich and famous one day, and then I'll pay everyone back."

"So, how long has Freya been at Hetty's?" I asked.
"About eight months."
"What are your long-term plans?"
"Apart from being rich and famous, just having a laugh. Live each day to the full, as if it's your last, let fate take care of the rest," she smiled. It was Katie's totally

unrealistic outlook that made her so appealing because she was so positive with it. She lived by her own rules entirely, and didn't care at all about anybody else's rules. She had created for herself total freedom and was lucky enough, it seemed, to get away with it. I asked her about Freya's father, whether she ever saw him. Katie lit up another cigarette. "Sometimes," she replied. I could tell by her tone that she had said enough, she didn't want to talk anymore.

We lay in bed together watching the sky getting slowly lighter outside. I felt totally in awe of Katie lying next to me. I thought this is one strong lady, a real survivor. Everyone else I knew, myself included, had done everything by the book. Done well at school, got good jobs to pay for the things we needed in life, and to pay for fun. Fun was at the bottom of our list. We had to earn fun; not so Katie. She lived for fun. Fun and freedom were her prime concern. I suppose I felt envious of her apparent freedom of commitment.

Chapter fifteen

Sunday morning, I think. We must have drifted off to sleep, because I woke up shivering with cold; it was absolutely freezing. I woke Katie up gently and suggested we go back to my flat and warm up before we died of hypothermia. We got dressed and removed the chair from the door. The hall was now virtually deserted, apart from a few crashed-out bodies here and there. As we left the house I glanced back at it, and thought what a beautiful place it must have been once, and wondered what the previous residents would have thought of the goings on there now.

My flat was really warm. I ran us a hot bath and made some strong black coffee. I found some clean clothes, an old pair of jeans and jumper of mine for Katie and a similar outfit for myself, and put them on the radiators to warm up. We both got into the steaming hot bath, and drank our coffee.

"I said too much last night," Katie said.

"No, you didn't, it was interesting, I wanted to know about your life. It helps me to understand you," I replied.

"I don't like you knowing too much though, it makes me feel vulnerable and I hate feeling vulnerable."

"Why does it make you feel vulnerable?" I asked, confused.

"Because if people know too much about you they can use it against you, and hurt you."

"I'd never do anything to hurt you."

"You say that now, but you don't know what you'll do in the future."

The telephone rang. I didn't feel like answering it, but it kept on ringing. Reluctantly I got out of the bath, wrapped a towel around myself and answered it.

"What the hell happened to you last night? I was looking everywhere for you." It was Niall.

"I'm really sorry mate, deserting you like that. We stayed the night in one of the downstairs rooms at the party."

"I could kill you for that."

"Hey, calm down Niall, what's up?" Niall sounded really distaught, not at all like his normal self.

"I'm in BIG trouble Jaz, I've done something really terrible."

"Slow down Niall, what are you talking about?"

"You know that girl you left me with, Candy, or was it Candice, something like that anyway?" Niall asked desperately.

"Yeah, Candice," I confirmed her correct name.

"Whatever, I slept with her Jaz, I actually had sex with her. It just happened, there was nothing I could do. I kept hoping you'd come and rescue me, but you didn't. She was so gorgeous, I couldn't help myself. We did it in a tiny room in the attic of the party; she was fantastic. What am I going to do Jaz, what am I going to tell Susie? You should have been there to stop me, I blame you entirely. Can I come and see you? I can't face Susie."

Poor Niall, he was in a terrible state. He really did love Susie, and to my knowledge had never been unfaithful to her before. This was very out of character.

"Sure, come round, we're just in the bath, but we'll be out soon. Give us half an hour."

"We? Is Katie with you?" Niall asked nervously. I told him she was and he changed his mind about coming round, saying he would go and face Susie instead, that he couldn't lie to her and that it would be best to get it out in the open straight away. I wasn't sure I entirely agreed with his philosophy, but he was in no mood to listen to reason anyhow, so I let it go.

"Everything OK?" asked Katie, when I went back into the bathroom.

"Yes," I replied, laughing. "It seems your friend Candice and Niall got quite friendly last night."

"Really?" Katie replied, surprised. I was surprised at her reaction; she seemed cross. She lit up a cigarette.

"I'm sorry I told you," I said.

"Oh, it's not you. It's just that Reuben was a really good friend and it just doesn't seem right somehow that Candice should be with anyone else so soon."

"She has to get on with her life though, a light hearted fling probably did her some good." That was the end of that conversation. We got dressed into our warm clothes, Katie looked great in my jeans and jumper. Both far too big for her of course, but she had put a belt on the jeans and rolled up the hems and sleeves, she carried it off well.

We decided to go for a walk through town and down to the river. It was a bitterly cold day, everything was white with frost and it was snowing very slightly, though not enough to make any great impact. We just crossed a very big main road when we heard this loud deep horn, and up pulled a huge, vintage, black hearse. Katie squealed with excitement.

"Spike!" she cried and ran up to the hearse's front-passenger window. I followed up to the hearse and inside saw a man with thin, long blonde hair wearing a battered velvet top hat. "Jaz, meet Spike, one of my favourite people in the whole world." Spike lent over to the passenger door which was by now open, and stretched out his hand smiling. I shook his hand and he suggested we jump in. I climbed in the back seat and Katie sat in the front. There was loads of room in the back. The hearse had been revamped to accommodate live humans. A large back seat had been welded in place, and behind that was a large storage area which was packed with boxes and bags.

"How are you, Cherub?" Spike asked Katie as we drove along.

Spike was in his late forties I would guess, a real old hippy. He had a friendly face with a permanent smile. His face had deep lines, a sort of weather-beaten look, and he had sparkling eyes which were very deep set. He wasn't especially tall and was quite thin. His voice was quite soft but very deep; he looked like a real character.

"Fancy coming to Wales?" he asked. Katie looked at me, smiling. I couldn't possibly go, it would mean being away for a few days, and I couldn't possibly leave the shop.

"Jaz, you have got to come. You've got to see Spike's place, it's beautiful. Up in north Wales in the middle of nowhere, a huge gothic house. If we leave first thing in the morning we could be back by midday. Surely someone else could mind the shop for you, just for the morning," Katie pleaded. She really wanted me to go with her; I was quite taken aback and, of course, easily persuaded. I could give Mark a ring on the way and explain the situation. He could do with practice in shop responsibility, but I wondered whether the shop could survive Mark's practising on it. What the hell, why not be a little bit reckless once in a while? I cautiously agreed.

So off we went to Wales in Spike's hearse, The Grateful Dead playing full volume.

"Jaz, you see that Moroccan bag in the back, can you pass it over please, man?" Spike asked me. I found the bag and passed to Katie.

"Inside you'll find some dope, skin up Cherub," Spike said to Katie.

"Whoah, Spike," said Katie as she pulled out a huge block of hash, tightly wrapped in hessian. "Been shopping have you?" she asked, laughing.

"Yeah, got four weights in there, I have to make these trips worth my while don't I!" he laughed.

"What else have you got in here?" Katie asked, rummaging around.

"Hey, I'm strictly a herbal man me, you know that."
"Oh yeah, and this is all for personal consumption too," said Katie sarcastically.
"So, I consume heavily!" Spike laughed. Katie cut off the hessian knot, cut off a lump of hash, and rolled an enormous joint.

It took us hours to get to Spike's house. I liked him; he was very interesting and entertained us all the way with crazy stories of his life experiences, including playing drums in a well-known seventies rock band, roadying with numerous other rock bands and travelling the world. When he found out I ran a comic shop he was ecstatic and was all for turning the hearse around for a private view of the shop's contents. He had Katie and I roaring with laughter most of the way.

Spike's house was out of this world. A real mish mash of archictectural styles. He had built it himself using old bits of churches, chapels and anything else he could get his hands on. The result was an incredible building containing stained-glass windows, steeples, stone-arched window surrounds, huge old arched wooden doors, church bells and some of the most beautiful chimney pots I have ever seen. Inside it was warm and colourful. Indian and Moroccan drapes covered everything. The rooms and shelves were full of interesting souvenirs from all his travels around the world. Outside he had a large vegetable garden. He also kept a couple of goats, some sheep, some pigs, and I was told by Katie that he had an insulated outbuilding somewhere where he grew hundreds of massive marijuana plants under artificial lights.

Chapter sixteen

Spike cooked us a wonderful meal with a wide selection of different dishes, and we sat at a long thin medieval table, drank wine, talked and laughed. It transpired that Spike was an old friend of Hetty's husband Simon. They had met in India where Spike was living in some hippy community which Simon had visited. Simon had gone to India just before starting university where he studied architecture. Simon being an architect and Spike, obviously having some interest in architecture, though a slightly unconventional one, meant their friendship grew and remained strong.

I sat and listened to Spike for hours. He was totally eccentric and great fun. He laughed about everything and was very laid back. He smoked hash continuously, like I smoke Marlboros. For every cigarette I lit up, he lit up another joint which he smoked almost entirely by himself. Not really being a hash smoker I kept to my Marlboros, even Katie declined after a while.

Our bed was a huge four poster with heavy velvet curtains and layers of feather quilts and embroidered covers. It was lovely and warm and soft, a great contrast to our previous night's sleeping arrangements. We made love and everything felt perfect. We were woken up by a cockerel at what felt like, and probably was, dawn. Katie got up and opened the curtains.

"Wow, look at this Jaz!" Katie shouted, excitedly. I pulled myself slowly out of the bed, wrapping one of the covers around me, and made my way over to the window. Outside there must have been a foot of snow. It was incredible that so much snow could fall in one night, but then we were in north Wales. My first thought was how the hell was I going to get back to the shop now, but Katie was leaping up and down like an excited child.

"Come on, Jaz, quickly get dressed! Let's get out there before it melts!" she insisted. *Before it melts?* I thought to myself, it will take weeks for that much snow to melt, and that's only if no more snow falls, which it probably will, and here we are stranded in the middle of nowhere, hundreds of miles from my baby who has Laurel and Hardy looking after her. I felt utterly miserable.

"Come on, Jaz, cheer up, I'm going outside." Katie got dressed. She still had only my jeans and jumper to wear, but this didn't bother her at all. I decided to get dressed and follow her out as there seemed no point getting upset about a situation I could do little about.

The snow was blinding white. It seemed so clean, not like the snow I'd always been used to in the city which was never white but a sort of muddy grey colour, and was more often than not slush anyway. This snow was completely different; crisp, soft white crystals, like in all those fantasy pictures on tacky Christmas cards.

Katie started making snowballs and throwing them at me, so I started making them too and throwing them back at her. It was really good fun and soon we were rolling around in the soft snow passionately. Then she would get up and try and run away laughing, and I would just about manage to catch her ankle and she would fall over on to the soft snow. We played in the snow for ages, jumping into snow drifts, building snowmen, then seeing who would be the first to knock them down, and having endless snowball fights.

Spike ventured out and asked if we would like some coffee. We went inside and sat on top of the Arga to warm up. Spike didn't seem at all worried about the snow.

"I'll get the tractor out, man, and take you to the train station in that." I asked how far the station was, and he told me about fifteen miles. Fifteen miles riding on a tractor in deep snow sounded like a nightmare, but Katie saw it all as a great adventure and was very excited about it. As for Spike, he made it sound as though it were something he did every day.

When Katie was out of the room, Spike came up to me and said quietly, in a very serious manner, that I hadn't imagined him capable of.

"Look after Katie, man, she needs you more than she thinks. She's really struck on you, I can tell. Katie doesn't fall for guys easily, believe you me, you're something pretty cool to her. I can feel the vibes between you. She needs help, man, she's one screwed up chick, and I can see her going down hill fast. She's lucky she met you, you might just save her from totally burning herself out. That cat's been through a lot of heavy shit, man, which she's never confronted, just blocked it out, and that's not healthy. All that scene with H and the smack didn't help either. She has to move on and get herself together, man, and get her beautiful little girl back with her too. Freya needs her mother, and Katie needs Freya too, although she won't admit it. Man, I wouldn't say all this to you if I didn't think you were right for her. I can see you're in love with her, man, and care about her. Take good care of her."

Katie reappeared. I was stunned, Spike seemed to understand her a lot more than I did. The mention too of H. Was H Freya's father? The same H I knew from school days, the description certainly fitted.

"Spike, have you got a sledge? Do say yes, I'd love to have a go, there are some great hills around here," Katie asked enthusiastically.
"Yes, I have Cherub, but we're going to have to make a move if you're going to catch that train," Spike replied.
"Oh, Jaz can't you phone the shop and tell them we're stranded and can't come back for a few days?" Katie pleaded.
"Tell you what, Cherub, I'll tie the sledge to the back of the tractor," Spike suggested.

It was still fairly early in the day, but Spike reckoned it would take about three hours to get to the station. So we had a huge fry-up breakfast of eggs, mushrooms, tomatoes, bread and Tabasco sauce and copious amounts of strong black coffee. Spike leant us a couple of heavy-duty coats to wear, and off we went. Spike, sitting up in the driver's seat as there was no cab, wrapped up so well that only his eyes showed, with a large joint hanging out of his mouth between the folds in his scarf. Katie and I sitting huddled together on the sledge behind, wrapped up in a large feather quilt.

It was great fun, though rather uncomfortable, occasionally Katie would push me off the sledge into the snow, giggling, and I would run after them and jump back on, or walk alongside Spike and smoke a cigarette. We had a couple of flasks of hot coffee with us which got passed around when we felt cold.

We finally reached what once must have been a road. It wasn't a main road and hadn't been gritted or ploughed. There was a car stranded; it had been deserted, but we had to move it to get the tractor through. It was a tough job and it took a long time to dig the car out and move it to the side of the road. I was beginning to wonder whether this was a good idea after all. Maybe we should have just made up camp at Spike's for a few days.

We finally made it onto the main road, though you would never think it was a main road, looking at it now. It was a foot in snow with drifts of up to three foot. As we drove along we met no other life at all, there were virtually no animals in the fields and no people around. Then up ahead a woman suddenly appeared out of nowhere, waving. Spike slowly drove the tractor up to her. She was standing by a car, very relieved to see us. "We got stuck in this wretched snow last night. We've spent the night in the car; there have been no people about at all. The battery's flat and we're freezing, thank God you're here!" she cried out to us.

Spike slowly got off his tractor to suss out the situation. He was far too mellow to panic, and simply lit up a joint and offered the woman some coffee before looking into the car. Katie and I got off the sledge to see if there was anything we could do.

Inside the car on the back seat were three young children, aged between ten and four all huddled together under a blanket, asleep.
"We were on the way to my parents for the Christmas holidays; I'm not used to the snow. I never imagined it could come down so thick and fast, my poor babies! My husband told me not to go, said the weather didn't look good, but I told him it would be better to go now before it gets too bad. He'll be worried sick about us. He was going to join us at Christmas in a couple of weeks. He told me to take the mobile phone but in all the chaos of leaving, I didn't pick it up. I know exactly where it is, it's on the coffee table, I can see it clearly, if only I'd picked it up. I can't believe I got us into this situation." She was really quite hysterical.

Spike gave her a hug and offered her the joint, telling her everything would be OK and not to panic.

Katie wrapped our quilt around the children and began rubbing their hands, while Spike, me and the woman began digging the car out. The children were very quiet, too cold to say anything, though the youngest began to cry. Katie started singing songs and telling them stories.

We eventually got the car out; it didn't take too long. Spike suggested I get into the driver's seat and steer, while he towed the car with the tractor. He didn't show it, but I could tell he was becoming concerned about the woman. Her fingers were blue, as were her cheeks, and she was shivering uncontrollably. She had calmed down a little but still seemed quite manic. It was probably the adrenaline pumping around her that kept her going. If she had slowed down I think she would have been in serious trouble; I was as aware as Spike about her fragile state.

She sat in the passenger seat drinking the coffee but was constantly checking on the children. Katie had done a good job in cheering them up, and they seemed quite perky now. The more the children cheered, the more the woman faded. I felt that as she relaxed about them, she let herself go. I kept looking at her as she began dropping off to sleep. I worried that if she went to sleep she would get dangerously cold.

"Spike we're losing her!" I shouted out of the window.
"Shit!" he said, but there was little we could do. The tractor could only go so fast. Then we saw a snow plough coming towards us. Spike got off the tractor

and ran towards it. It was quicker, after all, to run than drive the tractor. The driver of the snow plough radioed for help and came back with Spike to the car. Between them they carried the now unconscious woman back to the plough and lifted her into the cab and wrapped her up in thermal blankets. Katie and I carried the children to the cab. After about twenty minutes an army helicopter arrived, and with usual efficiency, dealt with the situation in an organised and well-ordered manner. They lay the woman on a stretcher and wrapped her in one of those silver sheets; they wrapped each of the children in one too, and airlifted them to safety. We unchained the car, pushed it to the side of the road and carried on our journey. The road from then on was more or less clear, the snow plough having recently cleared it.

After the incident Katie seemed very quiet; even Spike seemed more distracted than before. I think we were all in a state of mild shock. We finally arrived at the station. A typical Welsh station, built in dark granite stone, it consisted of little more than a couple of platforms, an old rusty blue-painted footbridge over the railway line, a ticket office, and a small cafe.

We discovered our train was running late, so headed to the cafe. I bought everyone a coffee and bowl of soup. We were all in need of a thorough warming up. Spike went to find a telephone to phone the hospital. He came back and informed us that the woman's condition was said to be stable and that she was suffering from mild hypothermia, and that the children were making a promising recovery. We were relieved to hear the good news I'd heard of stories like that on the news, but never thought I would be involved in one. I felt grateful that we had been there to help, but wouldn't want to repeat it again. Spike on the other hand, always smiling and mellow, joked about having to make a move, to go and rescue more damsels in distress. With that, off he went back to his tractor and the drive home. He was now wearing the coats he had lent us, as well as his own, which made him look three times his normal size.

Katie and I thawed out next to the coal fire in the small cafe, drinking hot coffee and smoking our cigarettes. I had given Mark a ring to check that everything was OK with the shop and explain that I wouldn't be back until late. He sounded in control and said that the shop had been quite quiet today, much to my relief.

The train finally arrived. It was an old, slow train with individual compartments with wooden sliding doors. It had no buffet car, and very few passengers. But it was warm and it would take us back to the city, with us only having to change trains once.

Chapter seventeen

We had a whole compartment to ourselves. We closed the door, pulled down the faded green shutters on the windows, turned the heating dial to full on, and cuddled together on one of the seats. Spike had given Katie some dope and she rolled a small joint. We relaxed and stared out of the window at all the beautiful blinding white snow. The sun was low and the sky completely clear, so everything seemed to glisten and sparkle. It all seemed blissfully still and peaceful.

Lying on the seat with Katie on top of me, I slowly put my hand down the neck of her jumper, fondling her warm breasts. She responded immediately, turned around and lifted my jumper up, began kissing and licking my chest. I slumped down further into the seat, as she moved her head slowly down my chest to my belly button. She undid my jeans and proceeded to give me a blow job.

I was in ecstasy when the door suddenly opened and an elderly lady in a hat and camel coat poked her head in. Katie and I glanced up at her momentarily but were far too involved in what we were doing to take much notice. She quickly realised her mistake and retreated closing the door hurriedly behind her amid mutterings of, 'Oh dear, oh dear me.' Poor woman, I felt quite sorry for her.

We changed trains onto a 'high-speed inter-city all mod cons' train and went straight to the bar and bought a collection of miniatures. The remaining journey was only forty-five minutes so we drank them in quick succession. I don't normally drink alcohol in the day, but on this occasion I felt I deserved it.

We arrived at the city at five. Katie and I said our goodbyes at the station and she went to see Freya and I went to the shop. I couldn't get there fast enough. It was all I could think about. Would it be in one piece? Would Mark have lost half the stock? Would Louise have been selling all the comics at the wrong price in her eagerness to help her poor overworked boyfriend? Would Johnny have realised we needed him to work today? There was, of course, no snow in the city and I felt sure that no one would believe my story.

When I got to the shop everything seemed to be running remarkably smoothly. The music was as usual, too loud, but Mark quickly rectified that the minute he saw me walk in the door.

"What are you doing here, Sarah?" I asked, surprised to see our Saturday girl here on a Monday.

"Mark gave me a ring, told me about your adventure. I just had to drop everything and come and save the ship." Very gallant of you I'm sure, I muttered under my breath.

"And what is that doing here?" I shouted in outrage at the enormous fake Christmas tree that had appeared at the end of the shop taking up half the room.

"Oh, that came with Sarah," Mark replied enthusiastically, always eager to please, before getting a sharp poke in the ribs from Louise.

"Well it can bloody well go with Sarah too! Sarah, thank you for helping out today but in future please leave your appendages at home."

"Coffee?" Louise suggested tactfully and disappeared out the back, obligingly offering to take my coat with her.

"Sometimes Jaz, you are such a misery," Sarah quickly added. I gave her a stern look, she turned her nose up in the air and went to stack shelves.

I went over to the counter to see Mark and go through the day's sales. Mark told me there had been a few phone calls including a few personal ones. Two from Niall, one from Susie and one from someone called Hetty. Niall and Susie's domestic quarrels I definitely didn't want to get involved in, but why had Hetty phoned? I was surprised she even had my number. I was far too busy to give them much thought now, it was the end of the day, I had only just arrived, there was a lot to do.

I stayed late in the shop; I felt I had neglected my baby and wanted to make amends. The phone kept ringing, but as it was after shop hours I felt sure it would be Niall or Susie, so I let it ring without answering it. I really didn't relish the thought of becoming a battering ram between the two of them.

It must have been about seven-thirty when I heard a loud tapping on the window. I got up and walked to the front of the shop wondering who on earth it could be. It wasn't until I got right up to the glass that I saw Katie holding Freya in her arms. Quickly I opened the door and let them in. Katie had obviously been crying and Freya didn't look too happy either.

"What's happened?" I asked. Katie couldn't hold back the tears and blurted out, without making much sense. "Hetty's thrown us out! I don't know what happened, she had a big bust up with Simon or something and accused me of taking them for a ride. I don't know, I thought everything was cool with Freya living there, Hetty's never been like this to me, I don't know what to do, or where to go. Poor Freya's had a terrible time." I gave her a hug and sat them both down. Freya was holding tightly onto her mother and wouldn't let her go. "Don't worry, you can both come and stay with me for a while. I'm sure what's happened with Hetty is nothing to do with you; she's probably just using you as a scapegoat for a problem Simon and her have. Maybe they just need some time alone together," I said trying to reassure her.

I closed up the shop and we walked back to my flat, Katie carrying Freya all the way. I searched for a suitable video and put it on for Freya to watch.
"I haven't got any of Freya's things Jaz," Katie said quietly to me.
"Don't worry, I'll take the van round to Hetty's and pick up as much as I can. You stay here and look after

Freya, you'll find some juice and biscuits in the cupboard," Katie stood up and kissed me.

"Thank you Jaz, so much." With that I went down the stairs and out of the building.

My van is no fashion statement but it serves its purpose well and has never, as yet, let me down. I got around to Hetty's in about fifteen minutes. When I approached the front door, I thought that maybe I should have telephoned first… what the hell I was here now. Simon answered the door.

"If you're looking for Katie, she's not here," was all he said as he began closing the door. This was all really odd. Simon and Hetty had always been so accommodating and friendly before.

"Excuse me, but I've come to pick up Freya's things," I replied.

"Oh, right, I'm sorry, come in." His tone changed completely and he seemed almost embarrassed. "Can I offer you a cup of coffee? Come on in and take a seat."

"Thank you, but if you could just show me where their things are, I must get back." Simon led me upstairs and showed me into a pretty little room, which was filled with pictures and mobiles and toys.

"Look, I'll help you," Simon offered.

The house seemed very quiet. There wasn't the usual sound of children running around. I wanted to ask what had happened, but the atmosphere was so tense and I didn't feel as though I knew Simon well enough. I thought the best thing to do would be get everything done as quickly as possible and get back to Katie. We filled two large cardboard boxes of Freya's toys and clothes and a bag of Katie's belongings.

"You can contact me here, if you find anything else," I said offering Simon one of my business cards.

"OK, thanks, bye," Simon said nervously. I hauled the boxes into the back of the van and drove off. There was definitely a strange atmosphere in the house.

Chapter eighteen

When I got back to the flat Freya seemed much happier. Katie helped me in with the boxes.

"You are so kind, Jaz, thanks for everything," she smiled.

"Hey, don't be daft, it's no problem," I replied.

It was by now getting quite late and Freya was very tired. We agreed that Freya and Katie sleep in my bed and that I sleep on the sofa. I tried to clean up the bedroom a bit. Putting all the comics in neat little piles, I began thinking of Trudie, and tried to remember how she had managed to make the bedroom look like a bedroom, not a scene from a frantic jumble sale. I picked up all the clothes and shoved them into the wardrobe, but the wardrobe door wouldn't close and they all fell out again. Did I have to fold them all up, every single one of them? That would take all night.

"Trudie!" I shouted out loud. Katie rushed in.

"What's the matter?" she asked. Then she saw me hunched underneath a pile of clothes and laughed. Freya followed to see what all the commotion was and giggled. Thinking it was all a game, she came and jumped on top of me and began throwing clothes all over the place. I gave up and let Katie and Freya sort it out while I went into the living room and lit a cigarette. The phone rang, it was Niall.

"How are you?" I asked.

"Terrific, Susie's thrown me out, never wants to see me again, or as she most eloquently put it, 'I never want to see your sordid, perverted, deranged, immature, squalid, impotent little excuse for a body ever again. Not if you were the last reptile on earth.' I mean impotent? I was never impotent! If I had been impotent this whole mess would never have happened in the first place," Niall said.

"And I suppose you pointed this out to her did you?" I asked trying not to laugh.

"Of course I did," Niall answered rather sheepishly.

"Well, you only have yourself to blame," I said unsympathetically.

"Look Jaz, do you want to come out for a beer, mate? I could really do with a drink," Niall pleaded.

"I'm sorry mate, I can't, not tonight. Katie and her daughter have just moved in, but you're more than welcome to come over."

"Moved in? Are you mad?" Niall replied in horror.

"Niall, just come on over and I'll explain everything."

"No, I'll leave it, maybe we could go for a beer tomorrow."

"Yeah, sure thing, I'll see you then."

I knew that Susie wouldn't tolerate Niall's infidelity and as good a friend as Niall is of mine, I don't think he really understands women. Katie came into the living room and closed the bedroom door quietly behind her.

"She's gone straight to sleep, poor darling," she said softly, helping herself to a Marlboro.

"So, what happened?" I asked, opening a bottle of champagne. We needed a drink and champagne was all I had.

"I'm really not sure. After I left you, I went to see a friend, Carl. Spike had given me a few ounces of hash to sell and I knew Carl would take the lot off me for a good price. Then I went straight to Hetty's. I was really looking forward to seeing them all, spending the evening with them, roll a few spliffs and tell them all about our adventures. But when I got there Hetty just started shouting at me, saying all these horrible things, basically saying I was using them and was ruining their relationship.

I was dumb struck. Hetty had never raised her voice in her life. Then she took her children and walked out of the door into the car. Simon just stood there not saying a word. When the door closed he just said he thought I'd better leave and not come back, turned around and went into a room closing the door behind him. No explanation, no nothing. Freya's really upset and thinks she's done something wrong. So then I grabbed Freya and our coats and left. I hadn't even said hello yet. I didn't know what to do or where to go, so I thought I'd look for you. I went to your flat but you weren't there. I rang the shop, but there was no answer, so we just sat on the green outside your flat waiting for you to come home. It was getting really cold and I was getting worried about Freya, so I decided to walk to the shop to see if you were here, but not answering the phone. What a relief it was to see the shop light on."

I handed her some champagne, we sat on the sofa together, and listened to some quiet music. Katie was very quiet and thoughtful, I could tell she was trying to work things out. We both felt tired, so I suggested she spend the night on the sofa with me, but she said that she wanted to be close to Freya tonight. This was a side of Katie I'd not seen much of, the caring mother. She did it as she did everything, beautifully. She suddenly appeared vulnerable but with a purpose. Like a child looking after their first pet rabbit who was recovering from an injury. It was as though she had become that child and viewed everything through a child's eyes, frightened and unsure, but desperately wanting to do the right thing.

Chapter nineteen

What the hell is going on? I thought as I awoke suddenly, in what felt like the middle of the night, to what sounded like the building falling down. In my sudden fright I had managed to fall off the sofa and become tangled up in my duvet, along with an empty bottle of champagne and a full ashtray, in the pitch dark. I tried pathetically to prise open my heavy eyelids, to try and focus on some order in this total chaos. Someone turned the light on, Katie was standing by the light switch, trying to conceal her obvious amusement at my wreckage.

"Sorry, did we wake you? You do look funny." She couldn't contain her laughter any longer.
"What time is it?" I asked, lying helplessly on the ground.
"You don't really want to know," Katie replied, laughing.
"I do."
"Six thirty," she replied still laughing.
"That's a time?" I replied in disbelief.
"Freya thinks it is. I'll make some coffee."

Katie went through to the kitchen. My eyes were just starting to focus and I looked around me at foggy images. There was a small dark figure standing in the doorway. I rubbed my eyes again and could just make out Freya leaning against the bedroom door wearing her pyjamas and clutching a teddy bear.

"Good morning," I said kindly to her. She ran into the kitchen and the safety of her mother. This all felt very strange. I climbed onto the sofa and Katie handed me a coffee. Then she took Freya into the bedroom to get her dressed. I looked around at the mess in the living room and thought that I really ought to get up and tidy the place if Freya was going to have anywhere safe to play. I pulled on my jeans and sweatshirt and began by collecting all the dirty cups and glasses and taking them into the kitchen. I peered out of the window; it was totally dark outside. I lit up a cigarette and drank my coffee.

Katie asked if I had any breakfast cereal. I never ate cereals, so there was none in the house. I realised some serious shopping had to be done.

"Here's some money, Katie. Could you go to the supermarket today and get all the things Freya likes to eat? I'm not really equipped with proper food."

"No way, Jaz, I can't take your money. I'll find somewhere to crash today and we'll be out of your way."

"Don't talk nonsense, you're more than welcome to stay here. In fact, I insist! It'll be fun having you both around. I need some food in the cupboards anyway, so please take the money and go shopping."

"You are so kind, Jaz," Katie said, then she came up to me and whispered in my ear. "I love you," and kissed me on the cheek. I was completely shocked and almost dropped my cigarette, but felt quietly very pleased with myself. I've done it, I thought, I've made her fall in love with me. Suddenly six-thirty in the morning seemed a wonderful time of day. Katie seemed embarrassed and quickly retreated into the living room.

It didn't take Freya long to start exploring the flat and find all sorts of things I'd given up for dead. Things like odd socks, half-empty packets of Marlboro and other such treasures. Things were definitely looking up.

Eventually it was time to leave for work. I kissed Katie passionately on leaving the flat. It was frustrating having her in my flat without being intimate with her. It was the first time we'd spent the night together without having sex, it felt odd. But hey, sex isn't everything. The main concern at the moment was getting Freya and Katie settled.

As I walked to work I realised that I quite liked the idea of Katie and Freya living with me. It had never worked out before; it didn't work out with Trudie, or the others before her. I felt though, that it would be different with Katie, after all, it was official, we were in love. I really don't think that I had ever been in love before. In lust, yes, more times than I care to admit, but never truely 'in love'.

Work dragged by very slowly; I wanted to get home as soon as possible as I think a tiny part of me was scared that she would leave and disappear again. But more than that, I couldn't wait to see Katie. It was a pleasant working day, at least I was so preoccupied with thoughts of Katie and Freya that nothing else really seemed very important. The result being that I must have seemed very laid back. Nobody asked any questions and I didn't offer any excuses.

The day was finally over. It had been a profitable, yet uneventful, day. Everyone left and I locked up the shop, lit a Marlboro, pulled my coat collar up over my ears, and made my way home through the bitterly cold wind. When I got to the flat I couldn't believe what I saw. The living room was completely clean and tidy, apart from a few of Freya's toys scattered around the place. Katie had put all the comics in the hall, had hoovered the carpet, and put everything precious or dangerous out of the way. She had also filled three vases with flowers.

"Jaz, I hope you don't mind. I just thought it would be best to get everything out of Freya's reach. I'd hate it if she damaged any of your things. I piled up all the comics and put them in the hall. I've explained to Freya that she is not to touch them, and to play only in here. I hope that's OK?" Katie said apologetically.
"Sure, that makes a lot of sense. Did you manage to get some food?"
"Sure have, and I've got a lovely meal cooking for you right now." Katie the domestic; this I had never imagined.
"You didn't need to cook," I protested. She slinked up to me like a sexy animal and kissed me passionately on the lips.

"Shut up and enjoy," She said and laughed. I wasn't going to argue with that.

Freya seemed quite settled, playing in the living room with her toys. I sat down with her and joined in with her games, chatting with her about her day. She told me that they had been to the park and fed the ducks who were, according to Freya, 'starving to death', and that they had been to the supermarket and she had helped her mum to do the 'food shop'. She also told me that she had chosen the flowers for me. This, it seems, had been her most important job to date.

I turned and saw Katie leaning on the door frame watching us playing together, smiling. Freya, it turned out, had already eaten. Katie had our food cooking slowly in the oven. She ran Freya a bath, and Freya got washed while I sat in the living room, smoking a cigarette, drinking coffee and reading a new edition comic which had been sent to me for approval. After Freya had been bathed, Katie dressed her in her pyjamas, put her to bed and read her a story. She then kissed her goodnight and came into the living room.

"How is she?" I asked.

"She's OK. Luckily Freya's pretty adaptable. She's had to be I suppose. I'm never going to put her in a situation like that again. I'm really going to try this time. I have a responsibility to her to be her mother. I've got a lot of making up to do. Anyhow, enough of this heavy stuff, food should be ready, are you hungry?" Katie put some music on, turned the lights down and lit some candles. She then brought the food in. It looked and smelled delicious. "I hope it's OK. I'm not a brilliant cook," she said hesitantly. I kissed her and told her it was wonderful and opened one of the few remaining bottles of champagne.

I had just finished the meal and was looking forward to an intimate evening with Katie when the phone rang. For the first time since I can remember I found it as soon as it rang. So, this is why people tidy up all the time, so they can find things. Suddenly it all made sense. Yes, I could definitely get used to my change in lifestyle.

"Jaz, why are you still there? I've been waiting for you for half an hour." It was Niall phoning from the pub.
"Niall, I forgot. I'll be with you in two minutes," and I hung up. "Katie, I completely forgot, I've got to go and meet Niall for a drink. Are you going to be alright on your own?"
"Of course I am, off you go, and have a good night. Say hi to Niall for me," she said laughing, knowing full well that she was probably one of the last people Niall would want to say hello to right now.

Chapter twenty

"I don't know what's got into you lately, Jaz. You were always the most punctual and dependable person around. I don't think Katie is a good influence on you."

"Hello, Niall," I answered coolly. "Do you want a drink?"

"I am seriously worried about you. Do you know what you're getting yourself into? And what about the shop? You weren't even there when I called yesterday. I have never known you take a day off work before. It's no good Jaz, you'll let the shop run down. What about taking on this child too? It's not your responsibility, mate, you don't want to be tied down to kids and all that. She isn't even yours."

"Have you finished? I'm a big boy now, Niall, I can make my own decisions. Of course I won't let the shop down, that would never happen, you of all people should know how important that is. As for Katie and Freya, I am in love with Katie, you ought to try it sometime, and Freya is part of the package, that's OK, I can handle it. I think it might even be fun. For Christ's sake Niall, we're nearly thirty, isn't it time we thought about settling down? Anyhow, I don't believe any of this is about me at all. It's about you and the fact that you've got yourself in a right mess, and you're just trying to offload it onto me. Well you'll get no sympathy from me. I knew Susie would throw you out. If you didn't want to leave, you shouldn't have slept with Candice, mate." Niall just sat there, staring at his glass.

"Oh, come on Niall, cheer up. Have you spoken to Susie today?" I asked.

"No, what's the point?" I had to agree, there seemed little point. Niall and I spent the rest of the evening in the pub. By the end of the evening I did feel quite sorry for him, and he was doing a very good job of feeling sorry for himself too. I got him a taxi and bundled him inside; he could hardly stand up, as I sent him home to his flat.

As I walked home, I wondered whether Katie would still be up. I crossed the green and looked up at the window, there were no lights on. I crept inside, all was quiet. I turned the lights on; Katie had tidied everything away. I looked in the kitchen, she had even washed up. This all seemed very strange. Katie hadn't struck me as a tidy-conscious person at all, and in bed by twelve, very odd. I peeped my head around the bedroom door, and found them both sound asleep, cuddled up in bed together. I stood and watched them for a few minutes, almost wishing then that Freya was my child. They looked lovely together.

The next morning began pretty much the same as the previous one had. It became clear to me that morning sleep was a thing of the past. Katie didn't ask me a thing about the previous night, she simply offered me a coffee and smiled beautifully.

"I don't want anyone knowing where I am, Jaz. People will start looking for me soon and I'd rather not see anyone for a while," Katie said as she sat down next to me with her coffee.

"Fine," I said, not really taking in what she had said, having not fully woken up yet. "How about I cook tonight?" I suggested.

"You didn't like my cooking?" was her reply.

"I loved your cooking, but I'd just like to repay the compliment. Besides if I cook for you, you have to be here, don't you?"

"Jaz, I'm not going anywhere, she replied. That reassured me. We hadn't actually discussed any long-term plans and I didn't know what Katie's plans were, if she had any. I decided not to push it, though, let her go at her own pace. Freya seemed to be settling in well and genuinely seemed to like me. I felt flattered.

After having a bath and getting ready to go to work, I kissed my 'family' goodbye and set off down the stairs, picking up the post as I left the building. There was a letter addressed to Katie. I ran back up the stairs and gave it to her. She looked at the envelope.

"It's from Hetty," she said opening it eagerly. I had a few minutes to spare, so hung around to see what it said. Katie read with a look of horror on her face. When she finished I asked her what it had said. "Hetty's left. She's taken the kids and is staying with her parents. Simon got busted with some smack. Simon doesn't even use heroin. He's really against it. He just smokes hash, never touches anything else, ever. Shit this'll ruin him."

"If he never touches heroin, how did he get busted with it?"

"That's it, Hetty thinks it's my fault, well not mine directly. Apparently, H came around looking for me and ended up spending some time with Freya. H is Freya's dad. Hetty thinks H was being followed by the drugs squad and stashed his gear in the house before he left. As he was leaving they busted the house. Of course they didn't find anything on H, but they did find the smack in the house and now Simon's been busted for possession of heroin. I can't believe it. No wonder they wanted me out. Simon must be furious."

"But if it's nothing to do with Simon, can't he just tell them that?"

"They wouldn't believe him. It's in his house, so he's responsible, that's the law, it stinks. I'll have to find H and get him to sort it out. The bastard, how could he pull a stunt like this? I hate junkies, they think of no one but themselves."

I was running late, I had to get to work.

"Katie, don't worry we'll get a good solicitor and sort it out. I've got to go, see you later." I literally ran to work. Mark, Louise, Geoff and Johnny were all waiting outside.

Chapter twenty one

I apologised to everyone; no one said a word. Louise broke the silence with her welcome offer of coffee. We all put our coats away and I asked Mark to put on a CD while I sorted out the lights. I desperately needed a cigarette as I hadn't had time to have one on the way to work, so I sat out the back and lit up a Marlboro. Louise was still out there making the coffees.

"You look tired," she commented. I looked at her and I'm sure she meant well, but I found her immensely irritating.

"Louise, what is it you actually do with your life?" I asked her.

"I'm studying economics at the university," she answered, proudly.

"That's what I thought, but don't you have to go to university to study a degree? Aren't there lectures and things like that you have to attend?"

"Well, yes, but I don't have to go to all of them," she replied. I give up. It was like talking to a vacuum.

I finished my cigarette and went through to the shop. There was a young man flicking through the comics. He turned around. It was Miles.

"Hi, mate, how's it going?" he said.

"Fine," I answered. "What can I do for you?"

"Well I was looking for Katie, I need to see her. I know you two have been spending some time together. Do you know where I can find her?" I replied in the negative. "Well, look, if you do see her, tell her to get in touch, it's important. Cheers mate, see you around."

He turned and strutted out of the shop. I could tell that Miles knew I was lying, but he had the decency to go along with it. I watched him go out of the shop, it was then that I noticed a tall, thin man wearing a dark woollen hat and dark trench coat, standing outside. They walked off together.

The shop was busy this morning and the customers were chatty and obviously getting into the festive spirit. I like the shop when it's like this. People talk, sometimes about crazy nonsense involving UFOs and green men, but on the whole interesting banter about comics, music and the like. It is on days like this that I really love my job; the interaction with the public and of course, the comics. I was a contented man indeed today.

Katie and Freya turned up. They walked over to me, Katie beaming. She looked radiant.
"I thought we'd come and surprise you," she said kissing me gently on the lips.
"It's lovely to see you. Have you met everyone yet?"
I introduced her to Mark, Louise and Johnny. She had, of course, already met Geoff. She smiled beautifully at everyone.

"Would you like a cup of coffee?" I offered Katie.
"No thanks, we're not stopping. We're on our way to feed the 'starving' ducks. We'll see you later," she

kissed me again and off they went, Freya waving enthusiastically at anyone who would notice.

All the staff had stopped in their tracks, as if they were in a game to see who could stay still the longest. I clapped my hands and suggested that everyone should wake up and do some work.

"She's nice," Mark said in a leading manner.

"She certainly is," I replied, much to Mark's disappointment. He was clearly waiting for some detailed explanation of my relationship with Katie.

"You could do with a good woman, Jaz," Louise helpfully suggested.

"Thank you, Louise, I'll bear that in mind."

It was lovely seeing Katie, she had brought an extra sparkle to my day. The trouble was that now I wanted to be with her. I wished that I was going to the park with them.

"So, is she a friend of yours?" Mark continued.

"Of course she's a friend of his!" Louise answered for me.

"Well, you never know, she could have been his sister," Mark replied.

"Don't you think that if she had been his sister we would have met her or heard about her by now?" said Louise.

"But we have just met her and heard about her. She could live in Australia."

"Why?" asked Louise.

"Because that would explain why we hadn't met her before," explained Mark.

"Mark, she's Jaz's girlfriend."

"I thought Rachel was Jaz's girlfriend."

"Rachel was never Jaz's girlfriend."

"Oh, who was then?"

"He didn't have one."

"Jaz, you did have a girlfriend, didn't you."

"Mark, shut up!" Louise snapped.

"Why? I'm sure he had a girlfriend, Jaz?" This was becoming quite painful.

"Mark, Katie is my girlfriend, Rachel is just a friend. Katie and her daughter Freya are living with me, OK," I said. Even Louise was stunned at this announcement.

"I think you'll find a delivery out the back, which needs dealing with," I said to Mark.

"Right. So you're saying that you've shacked up with that gorgeous girl and her kid, wow!" Mark replied.

Louise pushed Mark towards the back of the shop. Johnny caught my eye and grinned.

"Maybe they'll get a divorce and you can regain some sanity around here," he suggested and got back to the shelves.

"Geoff, did you get a chance to read through that new comic last night?" I asked as I had given him a copy of the same one I had taken home.

"Yes, I thought it was great. The graphics were spot on, the story line wasn't bad either, especially the bit when Shane faces the Thunderdogs without the help of the Fearsome Trio, while the intergalactic rainstorm is in full swing," Geoff answered with enthusiasm.

"So you think we should stock it then?" I asked.

"Yes, I think we should give it a go," he answered. So I rang the distributors and told them we would take it on.

Shortly afterwards the phone rang, Johnny answered it. "Jaz, it's Susie," Johnny shouted across the shop. Oh no, I thought, just what I have been dreading. I went over and took the receiver.

"Hello Jaz, I tried to phone Niall at work but he didn't go in today. Do you know where he is?" Susie said.

"Yes, he's probably in bed with a hangover. I was with him last night, he was very drunk. How are you?" I asked.

"Pretty bad, I can't believe he did it. He blames you."

"And you? Do you blame me too?"

"Not really. Well sort of, I mean if he hadn't gone out with you it would never have happened would it?"

"You'll have to keep him locked up in future won't you?" I replied, sarcastically.

"Jaz, I might have known you would jump to his defence."

"I'm not Susie. I just don't think you're handling it right. You can't blame me, nor can Niall. I didn't force them together. I wasn't even there. And for what it's worth, I think what Niall did was wrong."

"What's she like?"

"Not his type. Look Susie, I'm sorry, but I really have to go. You and Niall sort this thing out between you. Bye."

I didn't want to get involved in one of Niall and Susie's domestic scenes; they always ended up getting very intense. I was sure that they would be back together within a week and this little 'incident' will be the cause of umpteen arguments for the next year at least. I don't know why they don't just call it a day and be done with it. I was looking forward to returning home and began thinking of possible recipes for the meal that I was going to cook that night.

Chapter twenty two

Katie looked absolutely stunning when I arrived home that evening. There was nothing specific, she hadn't done anything different to her hair and her clothes were no different to the clothes she always wore, but there was something unidentifiable. It was in her face and her aura. She seemed to exude health and contentness. As if she had found some inner peace.

As I walked into the living room, Freya was sitting on Katie's knee and they were looking through a book together. The flat smelled strongly of freshly ground coffee, it was indeed a wonderful welcome home.

"Hiya, did you have a good day?" Katie asked, smiling and jumped up to give me a hug. "I've made some coffee for you," she said excitedly and bounced into the kitchen to get me some.

"Miles was looking for you. He said he needed to see you," I told Katie.

"You didn't tell him where I was did you?" she asked anxiously.

"No, but I think he guessed."

"Well as long as he doesn't know for sure, it'll be OK. Jaz, I really want to try hard this time and make it work out for me and Freya. I've decided to get Freya and me a nice flat, I'm going to stop the drugsand be a responsible mum."

"You know, I quite like having you both here. You don't have to leave, I'd like you to stay," I said.

"Yeah, but Jaz, this is your place, I don't want to intrude on your space. It's not big enough either."

"So we could get a bigger place, together," I suggested. She kissed me and smiled.

"You're crazy," she said and laughed.

But I was serious. I think we could really work together as a couple. I was completely devoted to Katie and I wasn't going to let her get away now. I could afford to support her and Freya, and with the shop expanding there would be more money coming in, it would be great. We could get a two-bedroom place, maybe even buy a small house, I could borrow the deposit and the mortgage probably wouldn't be much more than paying rent anyway. I had learnt though, that Katie couldn't be persuaded to do anything that she didn't want to do, so I would have to be patient, and subtlely convince her that getting a place together would be the best thing she could ever do. So I decided to keep my thoughts to myself for the time being.

Katie put Freya to bed and I started cooking. I had decided on a pasta dish with a rich cream and white wine sauce.

"Freya seems really settled here. It's so nice spending time with her. She's got such a great personality and she's so funny," Katie said as she walked into the kitchen and lit up a cigarette.

"She's a lovely child, you're very lucky, you know, to have her," I went up to her, put my arms around her and kissed her. She giggled and before I knew what was happening we were having sex in the kitchen.

In all the distraction the food burnt and was completely ruined. I suggested a take-away pizza, and we both ordered the most exotic and outrageous combination of pizza toppings we could think up.

I had one bottle of champagne left, so we settled down with our pizzas, champagne and a video to watch: the perfect way to spend a winter evening I thought. I asked Katie again, if she would like to spend the night with me on the sofa, but again she declined. It was so difficult to sleep, knowing that she was asleep in the next room, but I realised that it was important for Freya to have the comfort of her mother next to her.

We spent the rest of the week like this. I would go to work each day, Katie and Freya would go to the park, and every day when I returned home there would be fresh flowers in the house, fresh coffee in the pot, and the flat relatively tidy, considering there were two adults and a child living there. Katie never went out on her own, and as far as I knew hadn't been in contact with any of her friends, or taken any drugs. It was clear that she was trying as best she could to be the perfect mother to Freya, and dare I say it, the perfect 'wife' to me. It was fantastic having her around, she was always so happy and carefree. Nothing was a big deal, and we got on famously.

She still slept in with Freya, but we still managed to have a more than satisfactory sex life, in all sorts of places where I had never considered having sex before, not for any kinky reasons, hey, we didn't have a bed to share. We were pretty much undisturbed too. Hardly any of my friends were talking to me any more, and none of Katie's knew where she was, which suited us perfectly. We were living in our own paradise cocoon. Katie turned out, much to my astonishment, to be a pretty good cook. She loved all the comics too, and we would spend whole evenings reading comics to each other and discussing story lines, laughing at the far fetched ridiculous ones, and making up the endings to others.

She was a fantastic critique and had a really kooky way of interpreting things. She liked the comics with the female heroines the best and often we would act out scenes from them. She would play the part of a female super hero, and I a male villain, or I would be the super hero and she would be my side-kick. It was all very silly and light hearted, but fun nonetheless. That was how we spent the week, there were no heavy discussions, and I still knew very little about her. But it didn't matter, we were having a wonderful time now and that was all that was important.

Chapter twenty three

It was getting quite close to Christmas now, even I had to admit, with only a couple of weeks, at the most, to go. I decided that it would be a nice idea to take Freya shopping and buy a Christmas tree, and some decorations. Freya was very excited at the idea and immediately latched on to me. Over the last few days Freya and I had become friends, she had even asked me to read her a bedtime story one night, a great honour indeed, and every day when I returned from work, she would tell me in great detail all her adventures of the day.

It was midday on Sunday when we walked into town to buy the tree. It was another beautiful clear day. We had had no snow in the city at all yet and it was unlikely to be a white Christmas. Katie and I walked arm in arm and Freya skipped along beside us in her yellow wellington boots. I only had one Marlboro left, so Katie and I shared it.

Town was unbelievably busy. Everyone rushing around buying their Christmas presents, I was beginning to think this may have been a bad idea. I had no decorations at home, never having had a Christmas tree to decorate before, so I would have to buy everything from scratch. Freya thought it was wonderful and chose all sorts of unsuitable things to go on the tree, but with some gentle steering from Katie and myself, we managed to get some acceptable decorations, although I did draw the line at fairy lights.

We needed a break and I needed some cigarettes. I went to a tobacconists, bought two packets of Marlboros, and we went to a cafe for some much-needed coffee.

"This is the same place you brought us to that night the Christmas lights were switched on," Katie said smiling.

"I did make an impression on you, after all." Katie said nothing, she simply gazed at me and smiled.

"You know, I think I could be happy with you," she said out of the blue, holding her coffee cup up to her lips.

"I know I could be happy with you," I replied happily. She looked at me very seriously, but wasn't smiling now, just staring. Her eyes seemed sad and her face tense. "What's the matter?" I asked concerned.

"It really terrifies me, Jaz. I don't know that I can handle it," she replied.

"What's the big deal?" I asked confused.

"I don't know if I can let go, you know, give myself to you, trust you with my heart. I have such a fragile heart, if it broke I think I'd die," she said.

I had never heard Katie talk with such seriousness about anything before. I thought she must be joking.

"Well my precious I'm not about to break your heart," I said, laughing.

She lit up a cigarette and laughed too, and that was the end of that conversation. Freya was impatient to get the tree. Katie lifted her onto her shoulders and we continued our walk through town. I knew of a grocer's shop by the fountain that was sure to sell Christmas trees. As we approached the shop I could see a huge bundle of magnificent Christmas trees leaning against the wall outside. I pointed them out to Freya who climbed down off Katie's shoulders and began running towards the shop.

When we got there Freya was so excited she could barely control herself. I pulled a few of the trees out to get a better look at them. They were all different shapes and sizes. Some were small and bushy, others were tall and spindly, we were looking for something in between; the perfect tree. I eventually found two possibilities and pulled them out to have a better look.
"Which one Katie?" I asked. She didn't answer. I looked up at her; she had her back to me and was starring at the fountain. The fountain was approximately thirty feet away, but I could make out a group of about five or six people huddled around it.

"Katie," I said again, "which one shall we get?" Katie startled and turned around quickly to face me.
"Oh, that one, yes that one's lovely, what do you think babe?" she crouched down and cuddled Freya. Freya nodded with excitement. Katie continued to cuddle Freya, while I paid for the tree.
I came out feeling very pleased with myself. A mission successfully completed. Now all there was to do was carry the tree home and decorate it, it would be fun and I was actually looking forward to it.

Freya was trying to wriggle free of Katie's grasp, but she wouldn't let go. She had her face buried in Freya's chest. Eventually she let go, and gave her a big kiss on the cheek. Freya wanted to carry the tree, but I explained it was far too big for her to carry all by herself, but that she could help me by holding the end. Freya was skipping along bouncing the end of the tree on the ground as she went.

Having a child to share Christmas with made it all make sense. I was overwhelmed by the joy Freya was having over the preparations for Christmas. I looked up laughing at Katie, but she had fallen slightly behind. We stopped and waited for her to catch up.

"Can I have a cigarette?" she asked, quietly. I gave her one and she lit it up. "There's someone over there I've got to see, I won't be long. You two keep going and I'll catch you up," Katie continued. She then went up to Freya, lifted her up in the air and swung her around laughing. "I love you, babe with all my heart, and don't you forget it," she said kissing her and giggling. She walked off in the direction of the fountain and blew me a kiss. "I'll catch you up," she shouted smiling. I thought it odd, as I watched her, that although she was smiling, she didn't seem happy.

I looked over at the fountain, we were closer now, and I could make a couple of familiar faces. One was Miles, who gave me a wave, the other was the tall thin man I had seen him with the other day, whom I now recognised from my school days to be H. The others I hadn't seen before. I suppose she had gone to find out what it was that Miles had wanted the other day when he was looking for her, or to confront H about the scene at Hetty's.

Anyhow, she would catch up with us in a couple of minutes. Meanwhile, Freya and I had important business to attend to, getting the tree home and decorated.

"Come on Freya, it's getting cold. Let's see how fast we can get the tree home." By the time we reached my flat, Freya was tired and I was carrying the tree and holding onto Freya's hand. We got upstairs and Freya lay down on the sofa. I helped her take off her coat and boots, and fetched her a drink of juice.

Freya then watched me as I secured the tree in a bucket, and placed it in front of the window. I reached for the two carrier bags full of tree decorations and began getting them all out. On seeing the decorations Freya suddenly came back to life, and began, somewhat over enthusiastically, decorating the tree. She liked the idea of putting as many decorations on one branch as possible, so I had to suggest tactfully that it may look better if we spread them around a bit.

We'd been back home for about half an hour now, and still no sign of Katie. She hadn't caught us up on the way home and hadn't returned since. I wasn't too concerned; she obviously had a few things to sort out and Freya seemed not to have noticed as we were having fun with the tree. I thought momentarily of what Sarah would make of it all if she could see me now, and thought it was probably just as well that she couldn't see me now, she would never let me live it down.

Chapter twenty four

Freya and I sat on the sofa together admiring our spectacularly decorated Christmas tree. She loved it, and was fascinated by the shiny baubles. It would be such a surprise for Katie when she returned. I felt that maybe we should have waited until she got home to decorate the tree, but that wouldn't have been fair on Freya, especially as she had been longer than she said she would be. Freya began complaining that she was hungry, so in an attempt to distract her while I prepared something to eat I put on a video for her to watch. I had picked up her videos along with the rest of her things when I went to Hetty's. She settled quickly and I went into the kitchen to cook her some food.

I looked out of the kitchen window to see if there was any sign of Katie. It was dark by now, and I couldn't make much out except dark figures moving around on the green. I was beginning to become a bit agitated. It was getting late, soon Freya would be going to bed, surely Katie would be back before then? Freya and I had been back for about two hours, what could have happened to her and why had she not telephoned? Freya, thankfully, didn't seem at all concerned that Katie had not yet returned. I suppose she was too distracted by the excitement of the tree to give it much thought.

I gave Freya her food and when she had finished eating we played a game of Snakes and Ladders. I let her stay up for another half an hour, hoping that her mother would return in that time. She didn't. So I put her to bed and read her a story. She went to sleep immediately, I think the excitement of getting the Christmas tree had worn her out. She only asked about Katie once, which surprised me, but then I suppose she was used to not seeing her mother all the time.

I stood by the window in the living room smoking a Marlboro. I was feeling a mixture of annoyance and worry about Katie. I hoped that she was OK, and that nothing bad had happened to her, and at the same time I was feeling as though she had let Freya and myself down by not returning when she said she would, and missing out on the tree decorating. She had effectively ruined what was a very special day. There was nothing I could do but sit and wait. I was expecting her to bounce in at any minute, full of laughter and happiness and be completely astonished at my concern for her whereabouts.

I sat and waited and waited. She didn't come bouncing through the door. She didn't even telephone to say what had happened. I waited until gone midnight, standing by the window, watching. I tried to imagine where she was, what she could be doing and who she was with. The options were endless. Katie was certainly unpredictable. I had by now smoked my last Marlboro. I couldn't go out and buy any more because I couldn't leave Freya on her own. I concluded that under the circumstances the best thing to do would be to go to sleep; Katie had a key to let herself in, and it seemed pointless staying awake waiting for her to come back. I would be sure to wake up when she did finally come home. So I made my bed up on the sofa, read a comic and went to sleep.

Freya woke up in the morning with a shrill scream. I promptly fell off the sofa onto the floor. Then in my semi-conscious state, thought that I needn't worry because Katie would be there to comfort her, and tried to get back to sleep. Freya screamed again, and was now crying very loudly. I rubbed my eyes, and reached for the table lamp, knocking it over in the process. I managed to switch it on, Freya was still crying. I expected to hear Katie's voice comforting her, but heard nothing. I scrambled around for some clothes to put on, and got dressed, in a thrown together sort of way. By now Freya was almost hysterical.

I slowly opened the bedroom door, expecting to find Katie cuddling Freya, but instead found Freya on her own. I switched on the light and looked quickly around the room, but there was no sign of Katie, so I picked up Freya and gave her a cuddle. I managed to calm her down and gave her a drink.
"Mummy, mummy!" she was crying. I held her reassuringly and told her that her mummy would be back just as soon as she could be.
"Would you like to come to work with me today?" I asked. She nodded reluctantly. Then I took her through to show her the Christmas tree. This cheered

her up; she had forgotten about the tree, and seeing it again certainly altered her persona.

Once I had successfully calmed Freya down, I got her dressed and gave her some breakfast. While she was eating, I drew back the curtains and looked out at the green. It was barely daylight and there was a heavy fog hovering over the ground. *Where are you, Katie?* I said to myself.

There wasn't much sign of life outside at this time of the morning. I couldn't think what had happened to her. How could she have just disappeared? Apart from worrying me it was simply not fair on Freya. What was I to do with her? I had to go to work soon, and assuming Katie wouldn't be back by then, I would have to take her with me.

Sitting around brooding wouldn't do any good, so I chose some toys and books of Freya's and put them into a bag. I dressed her in her coat, hat and boots and left a note for Katie. I collected Freya's pushchair and we left the building and headed for work. I had no idea how this was going to work out. I could only hope that Katie would come and collect her soon - hopefully with a bloody good explanation for her absence.

We arrived at the shop, via the tobacconist, just in time. Geoff, Mark and Louise were already there, and Johnny turned up shortly after I arrived. I asked Geoff if he had seen Katie. He seemed surprised at the question and replied in the negative.

"Louise, would you be able to look after Freya for the day?" I asked.

"Well I have a lecture at two, but I could miss it, just this once," she answered. I chose to ignore her hypocrisy and told her how grateful I was. There was a large room upstairs, where the shop would extend to hopefully in the next few months, so they could spend the day up there. I took Freya up and got all her toys out and introduced her to Louise.

I came downstairs again and lit up a cigarette. I sat in the back room smoking my cigarette heavily, watching the kettle boil for the coffee. I held my head in my hands. *What was going on, where the hell was Katie and what was I supposed to do with the child?* Mark came in.

"Are you OK?" he asked. I just looked up at him and quietly answered that, yes, I was fine. I made the coffees and handed them out to Johnny, Geoff and Mark.

"So, how come you've got the kid?" Johnny asked.

"Well someone's got to look after her," was the only reply I could think of.

I told Mark to look after the shop for half an hour while I collected some supplies. He agreed and I left the shop, lighting up another cigarette as I left. I had to find Katie. I didn't know where to start. The last place I saw her was the fountain, so it made sense to start there. There were a couple of guys sitting around it, neither of whom I had seen before. I didn't know whether they knew Katie or not, but I had nothing to lose in asking.

"I'm looking for someone called Katie Crowe, do you know her?" I asked. They both shook their heads. Well it was a long shot. Next place would have to be Hetty's. Though I doubted Katie would be there, I thought Hetty might have an idea of where she might be. When I arrived there was no one home, and by the look of the house, there hadn't been anyone there for a some time.

I sat down on the doorstep and lit up another cigarette. How could Katie do this to Freya and me? Everything was going so well, we were all so happy I thought, she can't just leave us both. If I could find Miles he may be able to help, but I had no idea how to get in contact with him. There was nothing else to do but go back to the shop, maybe she had turned up by now. When I returned to the shop there was still no sign of her.

Chapter twenty five

By now I was beginning to feel quite angry with Katie. I had a business to run, I couldn't afford to worry about child care. I resented being forced into a situation of responsibility. My life, up until now, had always been in my sole control. That is the way I liked it, and that's the way I organised it.

Poor kid, it wasn't Freya's fault, and after all she was the one with the most to lose from the situation. I snapped out of my momentary lapse into self pity and began to focus on my work. Freya, for the time being, was happy and well looked after, so I could afford to put my energies into running the shop.

The shop was getting really busy, hoards of people filled the aisles. Johnny and Geoff were having a hard job of keeping an eye on all the punters and the stock, while Mark and I were rushed off our feet behind the counter dealing with the endless queues. I liked the shop when it was like this, it gave me a real adrenaline buzz. It is the closest I will ever get to starring in an action movie. How fast can I open the till and sort out the change, before Mark taps in his total? How quickly can I answer the customers' questions while putting the merchandise into the bags and tapping in my total into the till at the same time? Mr Dynamic, that was me, starring in The Assault On The Comic Shop, Oscar nominated three times for Best Actor, that was me, Best

Supporting Actor, that was Mark, and Best Film. While Johnny and Geoff played under cover surveillance officers, always on the look out, always prepared for any eventuality. Highly trained secret service men, also the money was good.

There was no time for anyone to have a lunch break on a day like today, but Louise came downstairs with Freya, they seemed to have bonded well, and suggested taking her out to buy some sandwiches. I had been so busy it had slipped my mind that of course Freya needed something to eat. I gave Louise some money and suggested she buy some food for the guys too. Freya was in good spirits; she had clearly inherited her mother's easy-going attitude.

The afternoon was as hectic as the morning had been. Business was good. Freya and Louise had returned and were playing happily upstairs, and the time flew by.

It was nearing the end of the day and I was operating on overdrive, serving two people at once, shouting coded messages to other members of staff, I was on a roll. The telephone rang, I picked up the receiver and shouted down it over the noise of the music and customers.

"Hello."
"Hello, Jaz, it's me, Katie. How's Freya?" There was a lot of interference on the line and standing next to the speakers, I could hardly hear her. I tried to move as far

away from the speaker as the telephone cord would stretch.

"Katie, where are you? What's going on?" I shouted down the telephone.

"How's Freya, is she all right, is she with you?" The line was very feint.

"Freya's fine, yes, she's here. Where are you?"

"I love you Jaz, you and Freya are the most precious things in my life." Katie sounded shakey, as though she was crying.

"Katie, where the hell are you, are you all right, when are you coming home, Freya's missing you like crazy?"

"I don't know when I'm coming back, please could you look after her for a while. Things could be so good with us, Jaz, you and me and Freya. You're the best, Jaz. You're too good, I can't handle it, it's all too good, too perfect, it's going to crack Jaz, I couldn't bear it. It's best to leave it while it's still hot."

"Katie, you're not making any sense. What about Freya? You have to look after her. Katie I love you, come home, I would never hurt you. Things can be good, it's OK."

"No one can take our memories away, Jaz. Let's not spoil things." The line became very crackly and we were cut off.

"Katie, Katie! " I shouted down the phone, but there was no reply.

I sat down, the receiver still in my hand. I stared into space feeling utterly helpless. The noise of the shop just faded into the background. All I could think of was my love for Katie. It was so strong and deep it defied all sense of reason. How could she think I would ever hurt her? It seemed crazy to me that she should want to end the relationship because it was so good. To me she had become everything, I would do anything for that girl, and here she was saying I couldn't because what we had was too good! It made no sense.

I had to have a cigarette, I dropped the telephone and wandered out to the back of the shop, Mark called after me but I didn't hear what he was saying. I sat in the back room in the dark and lit up a Marlboro, inhaling deeply with my head in my hands. I had to see her and talk reason to her, there was no way I was going to let it go, just like that. She needed me and I needed her, and Freya needed us both. I wasn't going to give up with out a fight, there was far too much at stake.

Chapter twenty six

I pushed Freya home in the pushchair, it was dark and it was cold. I had been preoccupied since the telephone call from Katie, I had simply been going through the motions. Freya was quiet and tired. We got into the hall of the house, Freya climbed out of the pushchair and I folded it up. She climbed the stairs to my flat, and I followed behind laden down with pushchair and bags of toys. I unlocked the front door to the flat and we both piled inside.

The flat felt cold and empty, I switched on the light and saw the flowers dying in their vases. There was a certain hardness about the flat that I had never noticed before. It appeared like a glorified stockroom; I suppose it had always looked this way, but I had never noticed before. Katie had made it a home, filling it with flowers, good smells and caring for it. It occurred to me that was probably what Trudie had tried to do all those months before, but her touch didn't have the magic that Katie's had, or maybe I had just resisted it at the time.

I fed Freya and put her to bed, reading her favourite story. I spent the rest of the evening sitting on the sofa, smoking, waiting and hoping that Katie would return at any moment.

I waited another day for Katie to show. Things had worked out pretty well with Louise looking after Freya above the shop, so we made the same arrangement for today. Katie didn't show up or phone and I was beginning to worry. I had to find her.

That evening when Freya and I returned to the flat I made Freya some dinner and while she sat at the table, I rang Rachel.

"Rachel, hi, Jaz here. How are you?" Rachel was no fool.

"Hello Jaz. What do you want?" she replied, to the point. I explained, as briefly as I could, what had happened over the last few days.

"Rachel, I need to ask a big favour. Please could you come around and babysit tonight. I have to find Katie. I'm sorry to have to ask you, I didn't know who else to ask."

How much humble pie can one man eat? I thought to myself. Luckily she agreed.

I managed to get Freya off to bed and shortly afterwards Rachel turned up. Perfect, voluptuous, humiliated Rachel. She appeared awkward and guarded. I told her how grateful I was and rushed out of the door, kissing her on the cheek.

"Good luck!" she called after me; I think she meant it.

I stood in the middle of the green and lit up a cigarette. I looked back up at the flat window and saw Rachel peering out. I gave her a wave and headed into town.

It was still relatively early, and I had no idea where I was going. I decided to go to a pub for a quick drink to gather my thoughts. I sat down at a table, pint in hand, chain smoking when I heard someone calling my name. I looked up, it was a couple of friends of mine, Ian and Sophie.

"Hello," I said, trying hard to appear calm. They sat down at my table and made conversation. I wasn't in a sociable mood and drank up my pint, made my excuses and left. I felt bad, Ian and Sophie were good friends of mine and I hadn't seen them for months, but I had things to attend to and I had to remain focused.

As I walked out of the pub I smoked my last Marlboro. *Damn, I'll have to get some more.* I anticipated a long night and bought three packets. I wandered aimlessly around the city centre, popping into all the pubs on the way, to see if there were any familiar faces that might know where Katie was, but without success. It was now approaching ten o'clock. The Dome would be opening soon, I would head down there. There was sure to be someone familiar there.

When I arrived there was already a long queue. *I can't believe this place, it's Tuesday night and there's a huge queue already, maybe I'm in the wrong business,* I thought to myself as I walked along the queue, looking for Katie. I could hear a familiar voice, I looked up ahead and could make out a man in a dark coat. I got closer to him and sure enough it was Miles.

"Miles," I called out to him.

"Hiya mate, be with you in a sec," he replied. He was talking to a couple of guys and exchanging notes, I stood in the background and waited for him to finish his deal.

"What can I do for you mate?" he asked as he came over to me, putting the notes into his back jean's pocket.

"Have you seen Katie, I've got to see her?" I asked him.

"Yeah, I've seen Katie, she's on a real bender! What the hell did you do to her mate?" he replied. I wasn't about to open up my heart to Miles of all people, but I needed to find her.

"Is she alright?" I asked.

"Look mate, if you've been messing her around, don't expect me to answer any of your questions."

With that he turned and started to walk off. I followed after him, rapidly losing patience. I caught up with him, grabbed him by the coat collar, dragged him down a side alley and pinned him against the wall.

"Look Miles, I'm not a violent man, but I need to know where Katie is. I've got her little girl at home, and I need to see her. Now are you going to help me or I am going to punch you?"

"Calm down you fruitcake!" Miles replied shaking his shoulders free from my grip. "First you've got to tell me the situation. You can't expect me to tell you where she is, just like that," he said. I took a deep breath, lit a cigarette and offered him one too.

"Ok. In a nutshell, everything was going really well between us, then she disappears, tells me she loves me too much, and leaves Freya with me to look after."

"Well that explains a lot. You have to understand Katie; I've known her for a long time; she's like a best friend. The trick with a best friend is don't get involved. Sure I've shagged her, but it was fun, nothing else. That's always been Katie's way. That way she's happy and everyone else is happy. There's a line with her, that you don't cross. You don't get involved, no demands, no expectations, just good times. But it looks like she crossed her own line for you mate, you've really got to her. Jesus, she's given herself to you, she's never done that before and I bet it scaring the hell out of her. It certainly explains her behaviour."

"But where is she, Miles? I've got to find her."

"She's hooked up with H again, and she's dropping so many pills, she rattles when she walks. Come with me, I think I know where she'll be."

What an unlikely ally, I thought to myself as I followed him through the dark streets. Miles seemed to know just about everybody, we couldn't walk down a single street without stopping to chat to someone or other. Some of them were friendly, some were hostile, others positively threatening. What they all had in common was 'business'. I kept in the background, not wanting to appear to be too associated with Miles, and becoming increasingly frustrated with his apparent lack of urgency.

"Miles, can we get a move on?" I asked impatiently.

"Yeah, don't hassle me, we're almost there."

Eventually we came to a side street that was very dark with no street lighting, it was quiet and littered with rubbish. *My God we're in hell,* I thought, but kept my thoughts to myself, for all I knew this could be Miles' idea of paradise. Miles led me up the street a little way, and stopped outside one of the houses, which was very rundown and had obviously been unoccupied for several years. We stood outside the old iron railings and Miles pointed down to the basement area, where there was a large steel door.

"That's where she'll be, good luck." With that Miles disappeared into the darkness and I was left alone.

Chapter twenty seven

I stood there for a few minutes and lit up a Marlboro, inhaling deeply. I slowly began descending the steps, when suddenly the door opened and two girls, very drunk, staggered up the stairs giggling, followed by a huge cloud of smoke that had escaped from behind the steel door as it opened. It all appeared very surreal.

I got to the door and gave it a pull, it was locked. I found a bell and pressed it, not knowing what to expect. The steel door suddenly opened and through the thick white smoke, I could just about make out a naked light bulb and the black shadow of a huge man. Nothing was said and I was pulled inside, with the door promptly being closed and locked behind me. *Well that was easy enough.* I thought to myself.

I could barely see anything through the smoke, but appeared to be in some sort of corridor. It seemed very small and I began to feel slightly claustrophobic. There were people everywhere, hot, sweaty people laughing chatting and drinking. Music was pounding away. Visibility was very poor and my eyes were beginning to sting. I pushed my way through the crowd, and entered into a large underground room. It was surprisingly big, for a basement, but then the basements of these huge old houses quite often were, having been designed to house kitchens and all the staff working them. The ceiling was high and the smoke much thinner, and although the lighting was pretty poor I had regained visual awareness.

I looked around the room, lit only by a few naked light bulbs hanging from antiquated flexes. Scattered around, in no particular arrangement, were bare tables and chairs, and people sitting at them conversing. It didn't seem quite so crowded as it had in the hallway. There were still a lot of people, but there was more space. There was a DJ at one end of the room, and a makeshift bar at the other, and the were people walking around carrying trays, collecting empty glasses and rubbish.

I wondered if this was what a Speakeasy would have been like during Prohibition. There were also a lot of drugs; people were skinning up, lines were being cut, and deals were openly being made. I realised now why I hadn't heard of this place before; this was seriously 'underground'. It was also very seedy; it smelled damp and was dark and monotone. I felt uncomfortable being there and was grateful that I was obscured by the thick smoke which, incidentally, my eyes had become quickly accustomed to.

I lit up another cigarette and began scanning the clientele, looking for Katie. I wandered slowly around the tables, trying to be as inconspicuous as I could. Nobody seemed too interested in me and I managed to move around unnoticed. There was no sign of Katie, then just as I was about to give up and leave I noticed right at the back of the room a table with two people sitting at it.

I stepped back to the wall and the shadow and peered at the couple through the haze. They were sitting on the same side of the table, backs to the wall, facing out to the room. They were very still, like statues, they weren't talking or laughing, just sitting, both smoking cigarettes. It was Katie and H. He sat tall, wearing a black brimmed hat and dark overcoat, pale face and eyes staring. Katie had dyed her hair; it was white, she was dressed in black and the sharp contrast made her look very pale. They were both motionless with a vacant air about them. There was none of the sparkle and joie de vivre that I had always associated with Katie; none of the instant warmth and beautiful smile. She appeared like a shell, as if her spirit had left.

Together, though, they had an incredible presence. They appeared as one, an impregnable pod. They appeared dark and dangerous. Their aura was quite amazing and they looked epitomy of cool. But they were cool, cool as ice. This wasn't the Katie that I knew and loved. This was a Katie without her soul. People were sitting near them, none of them communicating. H was holding court, totally in control of all around him. Everyone seemed in awe of them.

I stood and stared at them for some time, wondering what to do. Instinctively I walked forward out of the shadow, towards them. As I drew closer, H turned his glance slowly towards me. He saw me and stared at me. I stopped in my tracks. He took a drag of his

cigarette without taking his gaze off me, blew the
smoke out in my direction, realigned his gaze to its
previous fixed position and smiled slightly to himself.
I felt uncomfortable and turned to leave. I glanced
back at them before I left, neither of them had moved,
but I felt sure that Katie had seen me. She seemed to
be looking at me, but it was as though she was looking
through me, with no sign of recognition.

I turned and left; I couldn't get out quick enough. I
walked out of the door and ran up the stairs to the
railings, and when I got to street level I knelt over the
gutter and threw up. Gathering myself together, I ran
down the road as fast as I could. I ran and ran until I
got to the park. I walked through the park at a swift
pace until I found the bench that I had sat on the first
time I had seen Katie, playing happily with her
daughter. I sat on the bench, put my head between my
knees and wept.

I'd lost her, she wasn't my Katie anymore. I felt
broken-hearted and helpless. I hated H and I wanted to
hit him, hard. But I knew that it wasn't him who had
taken her from me, she didn't love him, and I doubt he
loved her; he was merely her escape ticket from me.
She knew that while she was with him I couldn't get
inside her, because she had become encased within his
void of drugs.

I hated her for it too, she'd let herself down, but most
of all she'd let her daughter down. I had never met
anyone with so much warmth and love to give everyone

and anyone who needed it. I'd never met anyone with such a childlike and unselfconscious sense of fun. She cheered me up when I had a hangover for Godsake; she made me feel great. Nobody had ever done that. Now look what she had done to herself.

I sat contemplating my situation for some time in the park, until I realised that my hands had become so numb with cold that I could no longer hold a cigarette, and thought that maybe it was time I headed home.

Chapter twenty eight

When I got home the lights were all out and Rachel had gone to sleep in the bed next to Freya. I went into the kitchen and looked at all the empty champagne bottles, memories of happier times with Katie, I dismissed them and made myself a cup of coffee. I clasped the warm mug in my hands and sat at the window looking out into the cold night, feeling weak and helpless.

I sat up all night and eventually watched the sun rise. It was a beautiful morning, with crisp blue skies. The ground was covered in a layer of frost and there were patches of frozen ice around. Rachel strolled through to the kitchen, bleary eyed and yawning.

"Did you find her?" she asked. I didn't turn to look at her, simply replied slowly,

"No," adding how grateful I was to her for looking after Freya.

"It was no problem," Rachel answered, "I had nothing else to do last night, and she was easy." I remained staring out of the window. "You look awful, Jaz, are you alright, have you been up all night? You really ought to go to bed," Rachel suggested genuinely concerned.

"I'm fine really, thanks again Rachel. I think I'll have a wash." With that I walked past her, took off my coat and went into the bathroom.

"Well I had better be off then," Rachel suggested.

"Yes, cheers Rachel, I'll see you soon," I shouted from the bathroom. Shortly after I heard the front door close.

I washed my face, brushed my teeth and combed my hair. I then walked into the living room and sat on the sofa. Shortly after Freya got up and joined me on the sofa. I gave her some juice and we sat on the sofa together with Florence, Freya's teddy bear, and looked at the newly decorated Christmas tree. Time drifted by, I didn't give a thought to work. The telephone rang, I let it ring. It was probably Mark phoning to find out what I was doing; I just couldn't be bothered today.

Freya and I spent the morning playing games, reading books and watching tv. The phone kept on ringing, so I eventually pulled the plug out of the socket. I was just going through the motions. I felt numb and exhausted, physically and emotionally. I knew I had to think seriously about Freya's future, and every time I looked at her I felt an overwhelming sense of responsibility. No matter how close I had become to her, it wasn't practical for me to look after her full time. Katie was obviously not in any fit state to look after her daughter and I had no idea when, or indeed if, she would ever be. Meanwhile, I had a business to run. Hetty had disappeared off the face of the earth, and Freya's father was a dead loss. The only option I could see open to me was to contact Katie's mother, but then that would really be going against Katie's wishes and I wasn't sure I could do that.

178

I felt angry, let down and betrayed by Katie. Surely the child's welfare was the most important priority. I knew what Katie would want and that would be for me to bring Freya up, which I would've been more than happy to do, if we were living together as a couple, but that seemed hardly likely at the moment. I would contact Katie's mother and test the water. If I felt it was right, I would hand over responsibility to her until such a time as Katie could look after her herself.

It all seemed too much to think about right now, today I would just take things easy, hopefully have a good night's sleep, and contemplate Freya's future with a clear head in the morning.

Chapter twenty nine

Freya and I had a special day, not doing very much, just hanging out in the flat. As soon as she went to sleep, I too went to bed. I woke up in the morning with a pounding headache and staggered into the kitchen to make a huge cup of intensified black coffee; I've found that coffee can do wonders on a headache first thing in the morning.

As I lay on the sofa, wrapped up in my duvet, the realisation of the seriousness of Freya's situation really hit home. Who was I to judge the future of this child I barely knew? I also realised though, that something had to be done, and that if Katie wasn't going to get in contact, then the decisions had to be made by me. I could think of no practical alternative than to contact Katie's mother, if, on meeting her, I felt she wasn't a suitable person to care for Freya in the short term, then I would have think of alternatives, but I had to explore that option first.

Freya came through to the living room, clutching Florence. She was a very easy going and adaptable child, and seemed to have become accustomed to the absence of her mother.

I reached for the telephone and dialled directory enquiries. I knew Katie's surname, and the town she came from was very small, so I didn't foresee any major difficulty locating her mother. The phone was dead. *That was odd,* I thought, desperately trying to reassure myself that I had paid the last bill. Then I remembered I had pulled the plug out yesterday. I found the plug, reinserted it and heard the reassuring hum of a happy, working telephone.

I got through to directory enquiries and discovered there were only two numbers registered under the name of Crowe in that town. It was going to be easier than I thought. I wrote both numbers down and hesitated, looking at Freya playing on the carpet with a jigsaw. I suddenly felt very sad. *Was I doing the right thing?* Maybe I should wait a little while longer to see if Katie would get in touch with us again. Then I remembered seeing her the other night, and remembered the shop. I also told myself that it needn't be a permanent arrangement.

I lit up a cigarette, took the phone into the hallway and dialled the first number. It rang for ages, I was just about to hang up when a woman answered the phone.
"Hello, Mrs Crowe?" I asked awkwardly.
"Yes," she answered, her voice was shaky. She sounded elderly and frail. Maybe it was the wrong Mrs Crowe.
"Katie's mother?" I asked. There followed a few seconds silence.
"Yes, who is it?" she replied slowly.
"Hello, my name is Jaz, I'm a good friend of Katie's. This is a bit awkward. I know you haven't seen Katie for a while, but I wondered if I could possibly meet

you, and have a chat about Freya." I was making a real mess of this, I really should have thought through what I was going to say. I wanted to hang up there and then. "Freya?" came a questioned reply, by now the poor woman was in tears.

"Yes, Freya, your granddaughter," I said hesitantly.

"Katie had a child?" Jesus, it never occurred to me that she didn't know about Freya. I couldn't stop now, I had to carry on. Taking another deep drag of my cigarette, I continued.

"Yes, Mrs Crowe, a beautiful daughter named Freya."

"Katie's dead," Mrs Crowe replied, barely being able to say the words. Things were worse than I thought between Katie and her mother.

"No, Mrs Crowe, Katie's been living in the city all these years. Look I really think we should meet so we can talk about things face to face. Could I drive out and see you tomorrow, maybe?" I waited for her reply.

After another long silence, she replied.

"The police came to see me, Katie's dead! They found her body yesterday. Apparently she'd injected some heroin; it was too much for her, she had a massive heart attack. She was dead when the ambulance reached her." I couldn't believe the words she was saying, I was choked as she continued in a methodical practical manner.

"If Katie has a daughter, she must come and live with me. Give me the address where she is staying, and I'll arrange for someone to come and collect her." I tried to pull myself together enough to speak.

182

"She lives with me," I answered and gave her my address.

"Are you the child's father?" Mrs Crowe asked.

"No," I replied and replaced the receiver, unable to continue the conversation.

I dropped the telephone on the floor and slid down the side of the wall until I was sitting on the floor, the cigarette fell out of my hand, and my eyes just gazed at the opposite wall, unable to blink. My stomach ached, my chest felt heavy and I could barely breathe. Tears began to fall spontaneously down my cheeks. I sat motionless for minutes, unable to digest the terrible news I had just been told.

"Daz, Daz." Freya called out. She had difficulty pronouncing the letter J and it always came out sounding like a D. I pulled myself together, cleared my throat and walked through to the living room.

"Would you like to go to the park?" I asked her, trying to sound as unfazed as possible. She agreed, so we got suitably dressed and left the flat.

I needed to get out and into the open air. I hadn't the courage to tell Freya the news, and the park seemed to be the only place I wanted to be right now. We arrived at the children's area and I sat down on the bench, while Freya ran off to play, giggling. I lit a cigarette and watched Freya playing, just as I had the first time I had set eyes on her mother. If I tried hard enough, I could visualise Katie playing and laughing with Freya, and just wished that she was real enough to come up to me and ask me for a light. Then I could tell her that she was the only woman I had ever loved.

Chapter thirty

Later on that day, a friend of the family came and collected Freya. I had packed all her belongings into two large bags as she didn't have a great deal. I held Freya tightly and hugged her, kissing her goodbye, I assured her that I would see her again soon. I wanted to go with her, to make sure she settled in OK, but the family friend was against it. So I helplessly let her go. It was more difficult than I thought it would be. She was the only real part of Katie I had now, but I kept telling myself that it was the best thing for her.

After Freya had gone, the flat seemed painfully quiet and empty, and I suddenly felt very alone. There was a knock on the door, I staggered up to it and opened it, expecting it to be Freya. It was the elderly Mr Simms, who lived on the ground floor.

"I've brought this up for you. Arrived in my letterbox a couple of days ago. Must have been put there by mistake. It's got your name on it see. Postmen these days, I don't know, don't train them properly, see. Now years back the postman would have known you personally, would know you weren't me. Anyhow, thought I'd bring it up to you. I would have done it sooner, only my sister Ruby's been staying, see. Well I'll be off now."

"Thank you." I replied closing the door.

I held in my hand a small white envelope with my name and address on it and a first class stamp, postmarked Monday, four days ago. It was in Katie's handwriting. I took it through to the living room and opened it.

Dearest, darling Jaz,

I couldn't talk on the phone, I'm just no good at talking to a piece of plastic, but I owe you an explanation and sometimes it's easier to write things down, don't you think?

Tell Freya I love her, I miss her every minute I'm not with her, but there's no one I would rather her be with than with you. Tell her I'm really looking forward to seeing the Christmas tree.

Jaz, I hope you don't mind looking after her for a little while, I know it's not easy with the shop and everything, but I'll be back really soon.

I'm scared Jaz, really scared. I don't think I've ever been so scared. This is so difficult to write. OK, here goes.

Jaz, I've never met anyone like you, or felt so much for anyone before. Hey, if I ever felt anything for anyone it always fell apart. My family fell apart, they were never there for me. Bess was taken away from me, the first of many, and my relationship with Freya's dad was an ideal that never happened. Everything I've ever cherished has been taken from me or left me. The only thing I have is Freya and I'm so scared of mucking that up that I can't handle being with her in case I do it wrong.

Then you came into my life, and made me so happy, and Freya too. You are the best thing that has ever happened to me, after Freya. I love you so deeply it hurts. Jaz, I want to spend forever with you. There I've said it. Really blown my cool now!

But then I think, what would someone like Jaz see in me? I feel you're too good for me, Jaz. I'm afraid you'll leave me. I couldn't cope with that, I think I'd die. A girl can only take so much rejection. Do you love me Jaz, will you stick by me and Freya? I don't know, and it's probably not fair of me to ask.

Do dreams really come true? Tell me Jaz, are the wishing stars real? I've been wishing on stars all my life.

I have to tell you Jaz. Last night I saw the Christmas lights, I want to take you, they are beautiful, they glisten and twinkle. You'd love them Jaz, we'll go down at midnight, when no one else is there, we could dance in the street. Will you dance with me Jaz, forever?

I'll be back soon Jaz, when I'm not so afraid. Maybe if I didn't care so much.

I just needed to say all these things to you, because I want it to work out so much.

I love you, always and forever,

Katie
xxxxx

I read the letter over and over again, until I could recite it, word for word, from memory. It was as if she were talking to me from the dead. I carry the letter everywhere with me; if it's not in my pocket it's under my pillow.

I went to see the Christmas lights at midnight that night, strolling down the street, cigarette in hand, I imagined she was next to me, laughing, smoking, dancing. *Yes,* I thought to myself, *Yes Katie, I'll dance with you.* I imagined I was dancing with her, her body close to mine, her smell, her smile, the soft sound of her voice.

Chapter thirty one

The time between Katie's death and the funeral passed very slowly. I went back to work immediately, needing a distraction. I hardly slept and the days seemed so long, that work had became a welcome time filler. I was there in body only, simply going through the motions.

It was a busy time at work, but I had lost my enthusiasm. Everyone was great, my friends rallied around to see if I was doing OK. Mark kept trying to do the right things, and Louise kept correcting him and apologising for him. Niall and Susie made sure I had a meal most evenings, but I wasn't really in the mood for company.

Miles came to see me one day. He looked pretty rough, not his usual cocky self and was quite quiet. He told me what had happened. Apparently it was H who had given Katie the heroin.
"They had both decided to do a shot of smack together, she had begged him for some. H hadn't taken into account that Katie wasn't used to smack, and gave her the same amount as he gave himself. Arsehole! H has been shooting up for years; Katie'd probably only done it once or twice, if that. It's no wonder it killed her. He could go down for it, if they can prove that he gave her the smack. But it was a genuine mistake, H loved her as much as the rest of us. He's completely fallen apart.

Anyhow, I'll see you around mate. I'm really sorry, I know how much she meant to you. She was one special lady. It's really tough on all of us."

The funeral was on the first Friday in January. It was a cold winter's day. As I drove up to the crematorium, I could hardly believe my eyes. There were literally hundreds of people there. I parked the van, got out and lit up a cigarette. I stood by the van for a few minutes just looking around at all the people. I had never seen so many people at a funeral before. I walked towards the door and someone called out my name, I turned around; it was Spike. He came up to me, spliff in hand. "Are you OK, man?" he asked. I nodded and put my head down. He gave me a pat on the back and we walked in together.

Inside the building was so full, many people were standing, squeezed tightly together in the hallway.

The ceremony was brief; a middle-aged man, possibly Katie's father, said a few words about her. Then some friends got up and paid tribute. Hetty had written a beautiful poem which she read out. Freya stood up and put a bunch of flowers onto the lid of her mother's coffin. We all sang a few songs and the coffin slowly made its way along the conveyor belt and through the curtains, out of sight.
"Goodbye my love," I said quietly.

People slowly made their way outside. There must have been five hundred people there, all people Katie had known and loved. All had, at some point, been a part of Katie's life. People mingled and looked at the huge collection of flowers which were laid out on the grass. I looked around for familiar faces; they were all there.

I saw Miles standing with a large crowd of people. Candice, Hetty there with her three children, she was wearing a large purple hat, and was obviously crying. I saw H, he was standing away from the crowd, with about four other guys who looked vaguely familiar. He stared at me with his cold eyes, but it wasn't an intimidating stare. He looked very sad and had a pleading look on his face. I turned away from him and saw Freya standing with a small, middle-aged lady with short black hair, who must have been Katie's mother. I went up to her and introduced myself. She was unimpressed. I gave Freya a cuddle and told her that I would see her soon. Mrs Crowe politely informed me they were leaving, and took Freya by the hand and led her away.

"Can I have an ice cream now?" Freya asked.

THE END

Made in the USA
Charleston, SC
04 February 2015